ENDLAND STORIES

or BAD LIVES

Tim Etchells

PULP FACTION LTD
PO Box 12171, London N19 3HB.
Published 1999 by Pulp Books, an imprint of Pulp Faction.
Copyright © Tim Etchells, 1999.
All rights reserved.

A CIP record for this book is available
from the British Library.
ISBN 1 901072 126

Cover design: Guerilla 6.
Photography (inside pages): Hugo Glendinning.
Photography (cover): P-P Hartnett.

Printed and bound by Mackays of Chatham.

ENDLAND STORIES

or BAD LIVES

Tim Etchells

Kings, lords, liars, usherettes, goal-hangers, gun-men and prostitutes,

Whether or not these stories bear any relation to life as it is lived in Endland (sic) is not my problem and good riddance to all those what prefer to read abt truly good, lucky and nice people—you won't like this crap at all.

Bear in mind it is not a book for idiots or time-wasters but many of them are wrote about in it. For the rest—concerning the bad language, bad luck and low habits of the persons described—I make no apologies and, like the poets say, "welcome to Endland" ©, all dates are approximate.

They replaced the lens in one (1) eye and I am waiting for them to do a operation on the other. Everything is fine. I am not an invalid.

Pax Americana,

Death to unbelievers,

Ringo The Anonymous, 1999.

CONTENTS

a small bad story in twelve good parts

About Lisa

The boss at DAVE'S TOPLESS CHIP SHOP is called Harry Stannington. The shop is just a franchise and the real Dave is more of a marketing proposition than a proper person. Harry Stannington is a pathetic lying police informant who's going to get his head kicked in and his tongue cut out, at least if you believe the graffiti which someone has sprayed up outside the shop.

#

Harry fancies a new girl that works in the CHIP SHOP who is called Lisa. Harry keeps asking her out but for at least a month she says no.

Lisa is basically an unlucky misery guts with a hidden gift for brilliant ideas.

Putting her top back on after work one day she finally caves in and agrees to go out with Stannington.

#

Lisa and H Stannington go to the pictures. They have to walk thru something like a forest to get there only there seem to be cats stuck up in all the trees—yowling madly and miaowing to get down.

When they get to the pictures Harry doesn't like the film but pretends he does.

Lisa also doesn't like it but can't be bothered to pretend.

#

It's one of those films where the plot was just a flimsy excuse put together to justify a procession of different sentimental conversations—at hospital bedsides, on dusky beaches, in empty offices and at tearful breakfast tables.

That night Lisa's sister gets murdered and Lisa blames herself—if she hadn't gone out it would never have happened etc.

#

Each day for a week Lisa has to wear her dead sister's anorak and other clothes to reconstruct her last journey. Lisa gets to be on television. She likes acting and wonders about making a career out of it. The people from the tv station have her typecast as the dead girl's sister though and won't give her any other parts.

#

Time passes. The relationship with Harry comes to a natural end and he sacks her from the CHIP SHOP.

There are no leads in the murder investigation except perhaps Mike Foreman whose arm is as thick as a porn star's penis (at least if you believe what the girls say) and who was occasionally having it off with Lisa's sister.

Mike hangs around in the Bull & Patriot Pub—everyone knows he's guilty but there's no evidence.

#

Lisa has a dream where she wins the Eurovision Song Contest singing a song in Portuguese. Later on in the dream she is back with H Stannington having sexual intercourse in the CHIP SHOP and he is imploring her:

"Speak Rwandan to me, speak Rwandan, I like it when you speak Rwandan..."

These kind of crazy dreams drive Lisa crazy.

#

One day Lisa sees Mike Foreman going down a side alley and knowing that the law is an arsehole and that Forearm is a murderer she kills him dead, with no regret. The Gods (such as they are) are pretty angry abt this and Zeus, Tesco, Venus, Mr Stretchy, Penelope, Kali and all the rest are all having a big row and making various wagers abt what will happen next.

#

The ways of the Gods are mysterious tho. Lisa isn't struck by lightning or by a satellite falling out of the sky. Instead her whole life just starts to go bad.

To start she has panic attacks, and many many long nights of sleeplessness. Her room is burgled (twice times), flooded (also twice times) and burnt a bit in a fire that is something to do with a bad persistent electrical fault.

#

Later (probably July) the automatic doors in all the buildings in the city seem to ignore her and no longer open anymore like they know she is no longer human or worse perhaps no longer a living thing of any kind.

Only by waiting for a stray dog to trigger the infra-red can Lisa get in anywhere.

#

Lisa gets more bad luck. She gets a skin complaint and falls out with her mum. Her new job at The Institute For Physical Research doesn't last.

Before long Lisa can't even see her image on the CCTV screens in town and she knows she's disappearing and she understands quickly that this is the punishment the Gods have meted out for her vengeance of her poor innocent sister.

#

People in the street try to talk to Lisa and try to act like everything is OK, but machines and most animals ignore her.

Lisa changes her name by deed poll. She calls herself something more suited to her age, race, sex and occupation. She calls herself SILENCE.

And from that moment on she lives up to her name.

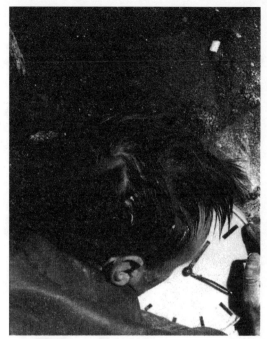

Shame of Shane

Once upon a time there was a mad biker, a dope
dealing Grebo from Derby called Shane. Shane went
in a pub where the barman's name was Meniscus on
account of how full he liked to fill the glasses
with shandy and ale.

Shane was a thief, a misogynist and an
intellectual pygmy. Meniscus was his friend.

#

On each third sequential Thursdays in the above
mentioned pub they contrived to run a semi-legal
Karaoke lock-in with Meniscus as the compere.

Such nites were a great laugh and indeed Shane
would gladly oblige all with a song. BRIDGE OF
THE RIVER KAWAI by Vermin was one of his popular
choices and his rendering of BUTCHER HEAD by
Carlo Verbatim Alfonso is still a urban legend
amongst the assorted biker scum and wanker
proletariat of that area.

#

SHANE + MENISCUS = TROUBLE, someone had wrote
up in the wrecking yard of a old factory in
Endland (sic) and this equation pretty well
summed things up.

GENERAL HOSPITAL, someone else had written on
the same wall.

TRUMP TOWER and YOUR FLESH IS NIGHT.

#

To tell the truth Shane never had much luck like for example the time he arranged to meet some biker mates to go to a disco:

Shane set off to the disco on foot but soon got lost and came to a clearing in the woods where a woodsman's cottage stood.

Nosy, full of fool's pride and lager, Shane went inside despite the signs which told him not to, and upstairs he found a beautiful woman asleep in a bed.

Shane thought his luck was in.

#

PATH BLOCKED BY SLEEPING PRINCESS——it said on the wall of the room, indicating the true nature of his entrapment——THROW A SIX TO CONTINUE.

Shane spent nine hours rolling the dice, unable to get a six in mounting frustration and missed the fucking disco.

#

Shane's bike was a souped up NORTON INTERCOURSE 650 and when he rode it in the mountains, with other bikers trailing behind him on their CARPARK COMMANDO 250s, then he felt free.

Shane had a woman (skirt) called Donkey on account of how many people had ridden her on the beach one night. Shane loved Donkey, at least so far as he understood the idea at all, and anywhere he went she travelled pillion on his bike.

Together with a load (outlaw posse) of other bikers they all went off in the hills of Nevada.

#

That night at Edale when the big hand was on the 2 and the little hand was on the nine Donkey walked a little way away from the pack at biker campfire and sat down. Shane went over and a argument ensued about the plot of an obscure slasher movie. Voices were raised and Shane was observed to strike Donkey and later, when he returned to the main body of the narrative, he was alone.

Shane was a murderer then.

#

Months, weeks and days passed and Shane fell out with Meniscus, partly abt the murder of Donkey and partly on the subject of 'interllactual property' (sic). Meniscus changed his voice to sound like Shane's, he cut his lank hair the same way too and when Shane had a tattoo done in big green letters on his forehead what boldly declared:

I AM THE ONE AND ONLY

Meniscus rushed right out and had one done just the same.

Meniscus was a moron, a joker and a failure. Shane stopped being his friend.

#

Round this time in Endland (sic) the King passed a decree to decimalise time. Ten (10) hours in a day there were then and ten (10) days in a week and approximately ten (10) long months in a year.

Shane was one of the many unfortunate bastards what lost his birthday in the changes and from that point on his legal (and mental) age stayed exactly the same.

#

Shane watched his friends getting older but no changes happened to him.

Bob The Biker got fat and got a beer gut. Jo Jo had twins. Clinton got busted. Twig got a job and Meniscus rightly got sacked from the pub.

He it was that nicked fivers from the till, poured chemical waste in a black bloke's beer and blocked up the urinals with bog roll, causing a huge eponymous problem in the gents.

#

Shane was still 25, you couldn't exactly call him a Grebo anymore but he still wore jeans and a dirty t-shirt.

Picture this: Shane with his stupid baby face while the rest of his olde crowde are pulling grey hairs from their genitals and sadly regretting the passage of 'decimalised time' ©.

#

Shane alone. Shane in the city.

Shane stood still at the cross-roads of time.

Shane reads all big books on human biology but it's no bloody good. His pals die and he's still young. Like a vampire film. He rides the bike but gets no kicks anymore.

#

Shane visits a Shaman in the shopping precinct near Hillsborough.

In the empty shop unit, next to that one that sells cheap types of broken biscuits, in the gloom of a fluorescent light he consults with this bloke, lighting a candle to the old Gods, speaking backwards language, squeezing drops of his own blood onto pictures of the Mighty Morphine Power Rangers and weeping in a Kleenex once owned by a cousin of the Queen.

All this to no avail.

Shane still 25 in Endland (sic), time stopped and 'future endless'.

A true story of earth and the gods.

Who would dream that truth was lies?

When the Goddess Helen and the God Apollo 12 gave birth to sons it was the talk of Heaven and the naming day for the twins (Porridge and Spatula) was a party that most would not easily forget and some would not easily remember. Wine poured out of the wine boxes like it had no end point and everyone laughed out loud and wore those necklaces filled with luminous yellow fluid what men sell on bonfire night.

Towards the end of day when the babes were asleep and all older Gods dozy with 'medicine' the younger Gods like Herpes and Vesuvius were fighting and dancing. The young Goddess Anastasia and a few others had opened their luminous bracelets and were flicking the fluid down thru the sky onto earth like a bright yellow rain. All over the world people were looking up and looking around—they knew that something wild must be happening in Heaven.

Now, upon the earth at this time there was living a very pretty girl called Naomi and as Porridge and Spatula grew up they both fell in love with her and made no secret of it—visiting earth and telling her so, sending flowers and fancy chocolates etc. In all aspects Porridge and Spatula were inseparable and friends—and they loved together to go joy riding, flying stunt kites and to funerals. But as time trickled on their rivalry over love of Naomi grew too great and they fell out, the one calling the other a complete lying cunt and the other vowing never to speak to that dickhead again.

Of course other Gods—Scalectrix, Fudge-Packer and Rent Boy—all tried to reason with the twins saying it was not godly to fall out over a woman thus and to get things in proportion—all to no avail. Only when Porridge and Spatula had a big fight in a Yates' Wine Lodge causing £100s worth of damage did their mother Helen intervene.

At her suggestion the twins agreed to stage a contest and that the winner of their contest would be free to woo Naomi while the loser would have to fuck right off out of the way and keep his bloody oar out. The principle of this she agreed with the boys, and left it to them to sort out what the 'exacting nature' © of the contest should be. In this detail did the troubles truly begin.

In Endland (sic) at this time there was a dire and miserable gameshow called QUIZOOLA! that by law was forced to play on tv each Sat nite at 7.30 til midnight on every channel and repeated on Tuesdays. Everyone reckoned that to win on this piece of shit was better than being King or in MENSA or like Albert Schweitzer. QUIZOOLA! went the catch phrase. YOU BETCHA! went the audience and the whole thing was a degrading spectacle whereby knowledge itself was rendered to be mere information and every human capacity and imagination were redrawn as stunted and thwarted lies.

Anyway. Porridge and Spatula decided to solve their contest over Naomi by going onto QUIZOOLA! and playing to the death. When word of this reached Helen and others of the older crowd of Gods they were dismayed for of course it was against the rules of the Immortals to compete in a human gameshow. Apollo 12 summoned the warring twins to his side and told them off asking them to abandon the dispute but both men refused.

Come the day Spatula and Porridge both had a lot to drink in the pre-show VIP lounge and argued, throwing jibes at each other and some other celebs. On screen and sat behind tawdry podiums the regular captains Fred and Rosie West introduced their guests/team-mates Porridge and a pale girl called Leah Betts on Fred's team and Spatula playing for Rosie alongside Joe Haldeman, a minor and allegedly corrupt govt official from the Nixon era.

Spatula and Porridge both looked very much the worse for wear and from the outset it seemed they were determined to outdo each other in bringing Heaven and godliness into general disrepute with the studio audience. At many of their jokes and lewd comments Naomi (who had showed up specially for the filming in a nice frock) had to look away and of the questions they answered most of the time they were wrong.

Spatula did not know who had invented invisible barbed wire, or what was the capital city of

Spain. Porridge did not know how many letters there are in an alphabet or even the name of the first black Pope. By the interval all crowd was laughing at them and Naomi was covered in shame.

As the tv played commercials for Baby Sham (fake kids), Porridge and Spatula threw water and then crisps at each other in full view of the audience and a scuffle emerged. Lucozade (who was King of the Gods at this time) took offence at this and finally decided to intervene, appearing in the studio like a flesh of lightening and causing an immense silence so great you could even hear the spiders spinning their webs.

In no uncertain terms he banished Porridge and Spatula from Heaven forever and told them off for using 'strong language'. The audience clapped and the host of QUIZOOLA! (some vermin bloke called Dick Turpin) thanked Lucozade for all his help and inspiration. "Never, in the whole history of 100 years of crap on tv have we had such troublesome contestants as them 2" he sed.

Banished in the night, slung out the loading bay doors of Shepperton Studios and bumping into a huge skip full of rubbish, Spatula and Porridge wept their first real 'tears of regret' © and the stars and satellites looked down and gave no pity, as was to be expected in those days.

#

Before long of walking through the city at nite Porridge and Spatula were set upon by merciless thieves who stole what little money, clothes and credit cards they had. "Stay your hand for we are Gods" said Porridge who was starting to sober up a bit but the robbers couldn't give a fuck if they were alierns from out of space or if they wore their underpants on top of their trousers or anything. "Shut up Fart Breath" said the robbers and "Avast Landlubbers" and "Chemical Cosh" and many other slogans of the day.

Shivering naked and with only each other to keep warm Porridge and Spatula looked like a couple of queer bastards going to a bent kind of party, holding hands and sobbing. Anyway. They soon realised they had to put their trouble and all disputes behind them etc if they were going to survive in the cold heartless exile of real earth.

Of how they stole clothes from washing lines to dress themselves in, of how they begged yen and Polish coins in the subway and how they slept in a gutter and a car-park, little need to be said here. And of how one night later they curled up inside the big big letters of a red neon sign to hide and shelter from the thick-falling snow not much need be said here either except to note that the sign bore the slogan:
JONESTOWN WHISKY: THE TASTE OF HEAVEN ON EARTH (which was ironic).

Suffice it to say that Porridge and Spatula did not die and they were lucky not to and that not being dead was their main achievement in all of three (3) months that passed following their terrible appearance on QUIZOOLA!

#

Let us now twist this narration to another of its subjects. While the banished Gods Spatula and Porridge wandered the earth all stripped of their powers and dressed in humble shellsuits, their 'truest love' © Naomi at first did not mourn their loss. She was a modern girl after all and hip to a different kind of beat so with the Gods out of the way she soon ended up going out with another bloke and took a job in the coffee shop at Woolworths.

Months of this passed—her cleaning tables and her bloke (who was a bit of a biker) coming in at the end of the shift and chatting to her as the male menopausal boss scowled on in disapproval. Naomi didn't mind the cafe—in fact she quite liked all the sailors or lorrydrivers what came in there and told stories of faraway places down the motorway which is like a freeway only not so free.

Anyhow. At a certain point things began to sea-change for Naomi so that for example she put on some weight and felt bad about her self and body parts. Also 1 nite Naomi had a dream abt living in America, near the border with Mexico. In the dream she had to cross the border every day—once in the morning and once in the evening—and each time she crossed it she lost something useful (a light bulb or a razor blade), robbing her of her heritage and will to survive. This dream upset Naomi no end and when she woke from it she decided to dump Bob The Biker and try to patch things up with Porridge and Spatula. She looked for news in the free-papers and made enquiries at some certain niteclubs and amusement halls where they used to hang out. All to no avail.

In point of fact, in order to save themselves from regular beatings, the brothers had been forced to adopt of more normal human names and henceforth went abt their lives under the aliases of Crispin and Gibson and thus, like the poets say, for all the world it seemed like Porridge and Spatula had disappeared. Together the ex-gods 'Crispin' and 'Gibson' had abt as much luck as ex-miners, ex-paras, ex-lovers and ex-cons tend to do (i.e. not fucking much) and in general fell in with a bad lottery.

If anyone asked them who they were and what the fuck they thought they were staring at, they were brothers and travellers from an antique land and they weren't staring at anything but only nice persons and minding their own business on a visitation to Endland (sic) in order to purchase up some parts for a oil refinery.

'Crispin' and 'Gibson' did their best to fit in with life in Endland (sic)—staying at a Unheated Salvation Army Hostel and drinking sake out of bottles still in the brown paper bags. Of local customs—Fire Walls in winter, Spastic Bashing and plays by Harold Pinter—the 2 of them were meticulous observant and both adopted the habit of smoking a curly pipe. Anyway. All this disguisery did not stop them being beaten and threatened or having their clothes stolen many times and of course no 1 would give them a job because their skins were as black as de-nationalised coal. Only at Xmas time did anyone show them any niceness when a few of the bus-drivers invited them round for Xmas dinner and a stripper or two.

New Year 96 for the twins was a real fucking downer, to say the least, moving on from town to town and upon the road again like Jack Kerouac, and wearing only Co-Op Jeans (blah blah). Together in their misery P&S swore each other a mighty oath/New Years Resolution that if either one (1) of them were killed on earth then the other would marry Naomi and look after her forever. How the brothers wept when they said this and the sad cars thundered by leaving them to the hardshoulder and rain, just by the on-ramp to the M6 at the Toddington Services, Bristol. Of all this, of course, cos she wasn't a telepath, Naomi was ignorant.

Time passed, phonecalls criss-crossed the world and babies were born, not much of it to do with this story or the lives contained herein. Only Naomi (long since neglected) on the whole planet thought much abt the twins. She tried to entertain herself in other ways—by getting addicted to heroin, by going to discos etc—but none of it really worked. Each nite she sat in her kitchen, drinking instant coffee that she made with hot water out of the tap and trying to complete a 500,000 piece jigsaw depicting a field of blood, mud and barbed wire at the battle of the Somme and in which every piece of the jigsaw was shaped like the body of a dead man. Still she could only think of Porridge and Spatula and she couldn't find 'restful sleep' ©.

One night, in her distress, Naomi called on the Gods for help, her hands shaking as she picked up the phone and dialled 0898 333 666 ETERNITY NOW and waiting through the various 'obscene' ads for other services until someone from 'Heaven' came on the line.

LOVE CONQUERS ALL said the bloke on the other end of the phone.

THE POSITION OF THE PLANETS SHOW A GOOD PORTENT FOR SCIENTIFIC RESEARCH AND MASS PRODUCTION THIS MONTH.

THE STARS ARE HOT HOT HOT FOR YOUR SEXLIFE THIS YEAR, he added in a thick Lancashire accent and an acting voice what bordered on the illiterate.

The next day Anastasia appeared in a shivering and shimmering vision to Naomi in her room. She helped Naomi a bit with her jigsaw (completing one of the really difficult bits which showed 3 blokes who'd been squidged by a landmine), exchanged diet ideas with her and then got round to the real point of her visit. Laying a map of Endland (sic) down on the table Anastasia pointed to it and told Naomi where the twin Gods had been hiding, their names changed and their faces disguised. Naomi traced red roads over blue rivers on the map, her finger joining places with names like Rotherspoon, Cardiff and Nigeria. That very afternoon she set off to find her friends, her few possessions packed up in the back of a car. Sweet Anastasia waved her goodbye and goodluck.

#

By this time of the yr (April) 'Crispin' and 'Gibson' were at their luck's end and surviving only by drinking rainwater and eating cardboard. Indeed 'Crispin' was working in a factory during the industrial revolution and safety was not its strong point. The walls of the factory were bedecked with slogans like LOOK BUT DO NOT TOUCH and WASTE NOT WANT NOT but this latter especially did not seem to apply to the workforce who were forever being maimed in interesting and barbarous ways in the machinery which, according to the management, was for knitting the tangles and knots of wire and wool that people sometimes see in dreams.

It took several weeks for Naomi to track the twin Gods down and for a while it seemed like Spatula/Crispin and Porridge/Gibson were always one step ahead of her. She tried the Bureau of Missing Persons and Tourist Information, and then in desperation hired a crippled detective whose compromised manhood was a kind of complex state-of-the-nation metaphor bound up with issues of contemporary polymorphous sexuality.

Ironside (for it was he) did a good job of helping Naomi and only charged her half the price he had on his business cards, smiling as he gave her the address of that hotel down near the Park & Ride Car Park where Spatula/Crispin and Porridge/Gibson were holed up. Naomi went down there early morning, the trees on the avenues all tangled in their branches with old audio tape and polythene bags hung in tatters.

When she got to the hotel Naomi bribed the bell-hop (three kisses) and then made her way up in the goods lift, hoping to be something of a surprise.

FREE KEN LIVINGSTONE said the graffiti in the goods lift.

MR BOOMBASTIC.

WHO WOULD DREAM THAT TRUTH WAS LIES?

In the room only 'Gibson' was there, lying in bed and watching a film called PIG TROUBLE (Soviet Kino 1935) while 'Crispin' was out at work in the knitting factory. Apparently even the actors on television stopped what they were doing in the middle of a scene and stared and started to cry when Naomi walked in and was re-united with Porridge/Gibson and apparently even the chambermaids in the corridor outside came running and danced and sang, and apparently even real rose petals ® fell from the ceiling and apparently luminous yellow stuff rained on the piazza from the heavens up above. N and Porridge/Gibson were overjoyed.

At six (6) o clock when Spatula/Crispin had not returned they were a bit worried and began to speculate a little in hushed tones. At seven (7) they were very worried and at eight (8) they knew for certain that something was wrong. At nine (9) there came a knock upon the door but neither Naomi nor Porridge had the guts to answer it. The person (or whatever it was) knocked several times, waited then knocked again but still N and P could do nothing cept sit still immobile there on the bed. They could hear the person get out a pen and paper and start writing something but still neither of them dare move to find out what was up. Their 'hearts were in their mouths'. Then after a while a slip of yellow-type paper came slipping under the door and footsteps of the person went stumbling away.

In a silence wherein you could hear the beat of a butterfly's wings Naomi got up and picked up

the paper, unfolding it hurriedly and handed it
to Porridge for she couldn't read. Porridge read
it out loud and for all its contents his voice
box did not falter.

The note said:

> The Person Crispin Killed in
> A Accident at UNilever
> sometime today. APologies.
> Sincerely...

And then there was a unreadable signature.

Naomi fainted and Porridge too felt a bit weak,
as tho one (1) half of him had been taken away
and would never return—like the cells in his body
themselves were 'rent asunder' © and like the
poets said, love, love will tear us apart.

#

A month of weird dreams. Rain clouds inside an
office building. A glass cat. Two kids on a kidney
machine. A man with dynamite taped to his chest.

In Porridge's dream (recurring) the Gods are
arguing about the ethics and codes of their
behaviour. One group maintains that since no one
believes in them anymore they are not obliged to
behave in any particular way—to set standards or
act like a mouthafuckin role model. A 2nd group
argue that godhood is an intrinsic quality whose
essence has to be maintained regardless of changes
in their perception (or non-perception) in the
outside world. In the dream Porridge finds himself

standing up suddenly to speak and crying out in passion thus:

"But surely fellow Olympians..." he says, "but surely this is just chasing shadows, surely this is just the old Stones/Beatles, Blur/Oasis argument all over again..."

The other Gods (esp Zeus) look to Porridge like he is out of his mind. He looks back at them and only after a minute or two does he realise the foolishness of what he has said.

Each morning Porridge wakes from this dream, covered in sweat, mouth dry, Naomi clutched to him, tears for dead Spatula in his right-wide-open eyes.

The Gods are just.

When Apollo 12 saw how much Porridge had suffered and how much he loved Naomi Campbell he said it was OK for him to be a God again and they had a big party up in Heaven and a wedding which is what all good stories end with. Anastasia was maid of honour and Rent-Boy was best man. All the Gods were there—Asimov, Golgotha, Vinyard, Hologram, Mr Twinkle and Horse Radish as well as Barbie and Jupiter and many others too. It was a fabulous day and neither tears nor fighting did mar of it.

Only at one point did anyone cry, when Naomi and Porridge slipped away from the main party for a while and went down to that pool in the forest through which you could look down onto earth.

There, thru the clouds and smog, they dropped a tear or 2 down onto the vandalised and unkempt grave of Spatula in Endland (sic). They missed him, of course, but kept their promises to him, and to each other, for ever and a day.

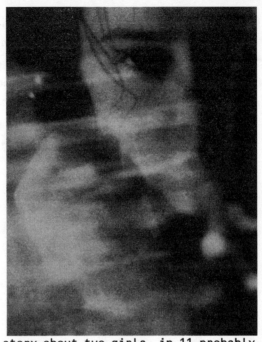

a very good story about two girls in 11 probably

religious parts

Eve & Mary

Eve earned money washing blood containers in a hospital and later she earned money by going round planting trees for the govt after riots in '81.

Yrs later she used to feel a gush of pride that the stunty wasted trees festooned with audio tape and polybag ghosts were all planted by her hands.

Eve could get pride from anything.

#

After a long courtship Eve got married to the son of a hairdresser. Eve (at that time) was a blonde Stripagram and he was a Tarzanagram and people sed they were a perfect match.

Some nites they stayed in together and practised their routines, drunk on gin and laughing like hyenas. Other nites they stayed in and assembled biros for piecework.

Times were good to them.

#

Eve and her husband/Tarzanagram bore one (1) kid —a girl Mary whose fave toy was a thing called MY LITTLE VOID. All night she'd stare in it, and all day if you let her.

Mary had what doctors called 'the faith of no faith' and many times dead birds, spiders etc were healed in her hands and their old tv worked better when she sat near to it or spoke and also she was double-jointed in an intriguing way.

#

At pay-school Mary soon got a reputation and her locker bore a big sign saying: THIS IS A 'PROHIBITED PLACE' AS DEFINED BY THE 1989 OFFICIAL SECRETS ACT.

Teachers avoided Mary and other kids were scared of her but secretly loved her. No one knew what went on in Mary's head.

#

Let us now change the subject.

At Mary's pay-school there was also a boy of the species called McGuinness whose hair was long and eyes roving (etc etc). McGuinness was so dumb he didn't even know he was alive. One day he got his hair caught in a new piece of experimental woodwork machinery (or something) and his head was damn near ripped off its moorings.

#

While McGuinness nearly died all the teachers and guards were in a panic and none knew what to do except switch on the school alarm bell and the sprinklers too and shout for help. McGuinness was rolling on the floor like a fish in quicklime, blood everywhere. The crowd that gathered was as clueless as it was voyeuristic and desensitised to violence. Mary walked thru the crowd, and it seemed (at least to those who were there) as if the crowd parted for her.

#

39

What next?

Mary knelt by McGuinness and took his head in her hands, fitting it back on where the neck was, cradling him against her and singing softly an old rebel song from the Spanish Civil War.

McGuinness swooned, and drifted and smiled, caught up in the rhythm of her voice and Mary smiled, a calm smile that most people only experience a few times in their lives.

When the doctors arrived at the school McGuinness was already better.

#

When summer came Eve and Tarzan got jobs in another town and Mary had to stay home in a Borstal. It wasn't ideal but her parents wrote letters every month which said the place they went to was cold as hell and ice froze over all the trees, cars and climbing frames in the parks. There were tigers there, and mammoths, and plenty of idiots too so there was a lot of work for Stripagrams and Tarzanagrams.

Eve and her husband got rich, slowly but surely, and joined the middle class.

#

Back home Mary did a few more cures and was soon pursued by the press and various cults. Everyone wanted to press the story of her miracle working into a story of their own devising but Mary wouldn't let them.

When a kid phoned up sick from a phone box or when an astronaut panicked on the long climb back down from space, when a train crashed and a passenger was caught, when a bingo-caller got cancer of the throat or when one of the lads on her estate got a hangover, Mary was always there to help. People soon called her God's Doctor tho Mary herself never believed in anything.

#

The days and yrs passed, getting faster and faster. Mary's life was like one of those gay musical numbers from a big Hollywood production only it was a kind of low budget thing and it wasn't really gay.

People said that each cure she affected cost her dear in physical energy and that sometimes she cried herself to sleep. If any of this was true Mary never let it show. Only the healing of a whole load of burn victims after a big fire at the local B&Q seemed to take it out of her and then only for a few days.

#

When Mary died (Winter 1640) her body was examined by the local constabulary doctor who, by reputation at least, was something of an expert in curios and women's anatomy. He found nothing strange.

Her house lies empty to this day and is often visited by gullible people from all over the world. No one can explain the strange rain of flower petals which falls there each year and still less the words which appear as if by MAGIC in the damp of her dark cellar walls:

PEACE PEACE, UNEASY PEACE.

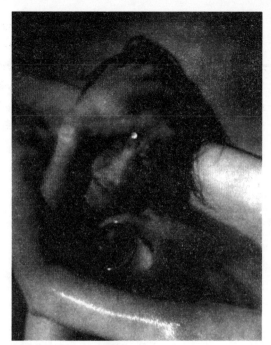

Cha~~Tkin~~wins

Chaikin bought a couple of girls in Endland. They were identical twins, the daughters of an upper class family what had landed on hard times. Sixteen (16) when he bought them and pretty to die for, with ivory skin and dark eyes, beautiful lips, the girls were also 'real virgins' © and Chaikin was pleased with that. Taken together as a pair (for the father wouldn't sell them as separates) the girls cost him £250,000 which is abt 2,500 Danish Kroner.

Elizabeth and Jane got taken off to his house in _____, where his wife, _____, also lived. Cheykin treated the girls real nice for one week while he observed them at rest and at play.

After one week (1 week) he began to perpetrate his plan upon them which went like this. He chose one girl and subjected her, morning, noon, evening and night to every kind of sexual act, perversion, demand and activity of which his mind and body were capable. The girl Elizabeth was, in this way, repeatedly raped, sodomised, whipped, prostituted, made to crawl naked on her belly through the house, made to suck the servants' cocks, used as a table for the eating off of food, made to stand for long hours half dressed and genitals exposed in the window etc etc.

And all this same time the other twin, Jane, was treated like a right royal princess, washed and bathed in Diet Lilt and made clean by servants, dressed in silk from H&M. Only once a day were the two girls allowed to know anything of each other, being kept in separate wings of the house—at 6 (six) each evening they were allowed to speak on the phone and tell each other their adventures of the day.

For six months this continued, the girl Jane cosseted and spoiled, falling asleep on Sweet Dreams pillows during massage 'by one of the many eunuchs in the palace'. And at the same time her sister Elizabeth crying herself to a bitter sleep with the sperm stains, soreness and bruises of some fresh indignity still aching in her body. What a great laugh this was for Chaikin.

Roundabout this time a bloke called _____ moved into the town where Chailkin held his domicile and opened a video shop. _____ was curious at the various reports he heard of the bloke who lived on the hill what had a wife and two apparently beautiful daughters or cousins or something staying at the house. So _____ from the video shop went up a hill to the house and knocked on the door whereupon Chaylkin's wife _____ opened the door and bade him to enter at his own will.

Claiming to be a traveller who had somehow lost his way from the ringroad and who was just trying to get to _____, _____ (the bloke from the video shop) was given a room in which to stay the nite and his horses were put up in the garage.

Falling asleep in his bed _____ was awoken

at midnight by a terrible screaming. He crept downstairs and saw the most beautiful woman what ever walked the earth (in his opinion) getting fucked in the mouth by a whole load of lunatics from the local asylum (or something) and each one with a member as large as his brain was small etc etc. Powerless to intervene, _____ went back to his bed and masturbated frantically before falling into a troubled sleep.

Next morning at breakfast _____ saw the woman again and, taking advantage of a temporary alone-ness asked her if she wished to escape from the Guest House with him that day. Imagine _____'s surprise when Jane (not Elizabeth) replied that she had no desire to leave the Castle and that her treatment there was every bit as fine and good as she might ever have wished it in a whole month of Sundays and that she was sure any other girl would give her right arm to be treated like she was.

Intrigued 'beyond belief' © _____ contrived to stay another day at the Castle by saying that his car still wouldn't start. He spent the day with Jane who, having been ordered by her master (Chaikins) not to mention her sister, did not and instead passed the time walking _____ (the bloke from the video shop) around the Rose Garden and making small talk in Latin, French and Greek as was the fashion at that time.

By midnight _____ (the bloke from the video

shop) was no closer to working out what the fuck was going on and he went to bed in a mood of confusion. An hour later he was woken (as he had been the night before) by the most appalling of shouts and screams which, on investigation, looked for all the world as though the gorgeous Jane with whom he had passed the day most refinedly was being enjoyed up the arse by a large black cardinal while a few buxom women in neo-Nazi uniforms (blah blah) held her down. Pressing his eye close to the keyhole _____ was so engrossed in what he saw that a noise behind him failed to register.

When Chaken's wife _____ tapped _____ (from the video shop) on the shoulder he jumped up at once and quickly made an excuse abt looking for a toilet and getting lost. Chayken's wife _____ told him where the bog was and excused herself, lighting her own way down the corridor with a long and unnecessary candle.

The bloke from the video shop (_____) made as if to go to the bog and then returned to his vantage point and watched 'Jane' getting enjoyment in several more kinky ways. After an hour _____ could bear it no longer and, utilising his memory of the House and its gardens, contrived to find a route into the chamber wherein 'Jane' was getting serviced. His route took him over rooftops, through windows, into ventilation ducts etc and left him finally concealed behind an old type of curtain made from psychedelic curtain material (called an arras) in the same room as 'Jane' whose cries of pain were pretty well drowned out by the groans of pleasure coming from a whole UK rugby team what had arrived.

Only when 'Jane''s torment was finished and she lay tired on her bed did _____ the bloke from the video shop reveal himself and implore her to speak with him abt what was going on. Of course 'Jane' who was really Elizabeth knew nothing of _____ from the video shop and thought at first his presence in the room was probably yet another cruel idea dreamed up by Cherkin. In the end, after much talking, everything got cleared up, the bloke from the video shop got a tearful embrace and together he and Elizabeth hatched an escape plan.

Just at that moment the door to the bed-chamber opened and Charkin stood in the doorway with his wife whose pale face wore a slippy kind of smile. Elizabeth fell on her bed in a dead faint and the bloke from the video shop, powerless to resist, was carried off to a high dungeon.

Several days passed in which the bloke from the video shop was kept imprisoned thus and it looked like he'd never escape. All he could think of was the indignities etc suffered by Elizabeth and the many hard-ons this gave him as well as how he wanted to save her and Jane. Only rats and other animals scurrying in the dirt of his cell were any company to _____ during this time.

Down in the town some of the people began to get a bit worried. The video store had been closed for several days and people were fed up watching the same stuff all the time plus worried abt overdue fines and stuff. Besides all this _____ had not shown up at any of his regular pubs and bars and he owed several people a drink. Remembering a conversation about the house on the hill (etc) one of _____'s pals organised a deputation to visit the place and search for news of _____.

Just when he (_____) was going to give up hope of ever getting out or eating human food again he looked out the winder of his cell and saw a torchlit procession coming up the road past Tescos twds the house. It wasn't long before the locals were barging down the doors with a couple of wheelie-bins and helping him, Jane and the woman Elizabeth to safety. How their hearts sang etc and blood soared.

All thru that nite (3rd Nov) Chaykin and his wife fled, trying to avoid mob justice but in the end they were caught and their bodies torn asunder and thrown in a river by the Volga.

People in Endland (sic) still tell the story of _____ from the video shop and Jane and Elizabeth and how they lived happily thereafter (nudge nudge) forever and a day and how the shop they ran was a good one (not like BLOCKBUSTER which rented out many many defective copies of

PINOCCHIO and CHAIN GANG) and how the Gods themselves (esp Zorba, Poseidon Adventure, Risotto and Mr Bumpy) were jealous of their pleasure and their lives.

AFTERWORD:

Chailkan's experiment on the twins certainly prepared them for a randy sex life but in many ways the results were surprising. Some readers have asked for details of how the two girls and _____ from the video shop 'got along' as it were and who was the horniest and most sexually adventurous and demanding of new forms of pleasure etc. However this is a good book and one that respects privacy and it is not an intention here to cater to the prurient and voyeuristic needs of that class of reader who, lacking such wild erotic events in his own life, would wish that he could read of them here.

SWife Swapper

Vargis was a kinky wife swopper. He swopped his wife for lots of things but in the end he swopped her one time too many and the bloke he swopped her with wouldn't give her back. That was in 1970 but all dates are approximate.

Poor Vargis. To him, from then on, the earth was nothing but a charred desolate cinder wasteland floating in space.

#

Vargis started to sell Tupperware. He sniffed lighter fluid. He went out with men that wore women's clothes. He read 'poetic books' © with BIG WORDS. He payed a woman to urinate on him, but nothing could cure him of his love for that wife.

When the sun set over the cooling towers Vargis took no pleasure in it. When a baby was born Vargis didn't care. When the tv showed pics of 'newly discovered heaven' he thought it was a con.

#

At last, in desperation, Vargis called many wise men and viziers abt him and asked them what to do. Some said he should revoke the fucking Poll Tax, others said he should fast for ninety (90) days and still others said he should pull his bloody finger out. All these persons Vargis dispatched unto their deaths, showing 'no mercy' © as was the way for such persons then.

#

Last of all a girl called Chantalle came to Vargis. She was a girl who worked the eight til late shift at EIGHT TILL LATE and she was cross-eyed and Vargis had a thing for cross-eyed girls; he just couldn't help it.

Chantalle told him he had to 'leave the kingdom' as a penance and go to Persia which was a country that didn't exist anymore—only then would he see his beloved wife again.

\#

Vargis understood little of what was said to him by Chantalle—he didn't understand how you could go to a country that didn't exist anymore and he didn't understand the idea of a kingdom and he made many other pedantic objections. In the end tho he agreed to make the journey and bought a new jumper especially.

\#

Night before he left, Vargis hired a funfair just for himself and all his mates only the funfair was kind of freaky and the rides all had ominous names like WHEEL OF MISFORTUNE, TUNNEL OF BLOOD & TRAVEL SICKNESS. Vargis got caught in the turnstile for the HELL-TER-SKELL-TER and the firemen with welding equipment had to cut him out.

\#

The plane left at midnight or dawn and for some

reason the inflight movie was a vicious kung-fu slashathon with dialogue in the Philippine language Tagalog. The flight to 'Persia' lasted six hours but the film lasted nine hours and so when they landed at Persia International, the captain and that made everyone stay on board until the movie was finished. Three hours they sat on the tarmac, watching murderous acts of barefisted human carnage, while the cabin crew roared and drank and cheered duty free.

#

Once, in the background of a scene, Vargis thought he glimpsed his wife looking sadly at the ground but he was certainly mistaken.

Vargis had his papers all in order. He had a passport, a visa and a letter with his address printed on it. When he got to the customs the black bloke just waved him through.

#

Persia was more of a state of mind than an actual place and time seemed to pass there very slowly or else not at all.

To Vargis the city he found himself in was experienced only as a series of flashes—hot bursts on his retina like the unforgettable images seen by soldiers shot by the new Russian Dream Rifle ©. Persia was Frankincense purchased from an ancient subway vending machine. It was oil

dripping from the roof. It was three week old
copies of the National Front rhyming newspaper BAD
NEWS FOR THE JEWS.

Vargis found it hard to keep up with news from
home.

#

For three weeks nothing roused Vargis from the
stupor above described and then the phone rang in
his hotel room and he was speaking to his wife.

"Persephone" he said.

"Yes" she said.

"I missed you" he said.

"Yes" she said and then, as the poets say, they
cried together, and were 'unable to find words'.

#

In hours of the phonecall they were reunited and
she was in his arms and he in hers (etc) and she
said they'd never be parted again and that was
half true.

Before they could leave Vargis had to answer
riddles put up by the hotel management. There was
one abt ten men mowing a meadow, there was another
on abt sixteen (16) jars full of water and a crow
dropping stones in there. There was one abt the
England World Cup Squad of 1962.

But Vargis knew all the answers and Persephone
was a good listener.

#

Vargis and Persephone sat on the plane and looked out the windows as it took off. They liked the way the clouds were sculpted into beautiful shapes. They liked the way the stewards demonstrated all safety routines. And they loved the way the plane rolled and fell over Lockerbie.

They were never parted in the rest of their short lives.

James

Old days

It was November and cold. James thought he did not like a nite picnic and in the hurry to get into the car when the thunder really started he dropped KANGAROO and no one could find him in the dark. So then KANGAROO was lost and James only had DEAD SOLDIER to play with.

For the nite picnic, Dad had stretched the blanket on the concrete near them old trees and the hi-rises with shell holes in them what looked like a skull and they all sat and Harry cried and Olivia saw that scary ghosts were stealing crisps from them when they looked away. That was when the thunder started.

They ate by the lite of car headlights and somehow pretended not to notice that Dad was slowly slowly slowly losing the plot.

#

In the car journey to home James said he was frightened.

Dad asked him 'why?'.

And James said 'the dark'.

And then it was all quiet in the car and you could hear the rain and you could hear the moaning sound that DEAD SOLDIER makes sometimes when no one plays with him and James waited a very long time for someone to say something and he waited and he waited and he waited and no one did.

They drove over Scary Mountain, thru the woods and the 'sound of trees' ©.

James asked: 'Who can sing a song to un-frighten me?'

Dad didn't say nothing.

And Olivia was quiet. And Harry was too little to really understand the question. And Mum was long gone. And there was no one else in the car.

#

After the nite picnic things calmed down a bit (approx 1 month) and in any case Dad was back at work, in a big white building* with long corridors that was always smelling of disinfectant and the kids went back to school.

School was more corridors and also concrete and metal detectors, strange rulers and rationing, learning songs and actions to go with them and J made a picture every day.

Pictures:

Planets.

A jungle.

Gunship.

A robot on fire.

Space vehicle.

Sky.

There was a picture of Dad too—a blunt try at painting something tangible of J's world but Dad

(* probably a hospital or morgue)

in the picture was blurred and waterlogged,
lacking definition. Dad swamped in the green blue
colour of bad dreams.

#

A week or 2 passed. J and O learned stuff at the
school, Harry cried and Dad bought an illegal
patch for DOOM that changed the faces on all of
the monsters stalking its dark green corridors
into his own face. No one mentioned the nite-
picnic, no one mentioned the rain which really
seemed to start on that nite and never found time
to stop. And no one mentioned the loss of
KANGAROO.

Dad's patch for DOOM was a passport picture for
the country of distortion and death, scanned in
and replicated a thousand times so that in the
hours and hours of his playing he killed himself
a million times, splattering his own blood to four
corners but playing and playing again. Dad all
fucked out with lack of sleep, his own face
wounded in the mirror of the screen.

There were no more nite picnics and no more
songs. There were no more phone calls from Mum.
But there was a spider web of tension in the house
where the curtains were always closed, a spider
web of tension linking everything, wound tite
between the furniture and caught into their
clothes.

One morning Olivia found Dad crying again at

the breakfast table—there was a gun (or something shaped like one) in his hands. She were too scared to tell anyone.

#

Some conversations.
   (a) Do you think he'll make it type stuff.
J pessimistic. O trying hard. Harry just crying.
   (b) On the nature of physical reality.
   J asking O questions. A dream he had one nite about a man whose eyes were spinning saucers like an olden cartoon.

#

Daze of school daze. In biology O closed her book (a picture of dissected twins) and walked with Mrs _____ to the office, not knowing what to expect but knowing that the world was changed or changing as she walked. Outside the office was the usual collection of children that could be found there, many of them wearing dunces caps and J too (but not wearing one). O coughed and the dunces sniffed or looked bored or whatsoever they supposed might be best and O sat down besides J and the 2 waited.
   In the office J asked what it was and Mrs _____ said their Dad was not feeling well and flipped out at the factory and hospitalised in tears and was there maybe someone else who could look after them for a while?

Olivia shook her head. Mrs _____ made a phone call.

And then the new days began.

New days

Just down the road from the orphanage there was a tall electricity pylon that were strictly out of bounds and 'that cold winter' © in particular a huge plastic sheet half turned to tatters had caught in the bottom of the pylon tower. To James, stood at the window of the orphanage, this black polythene tangle, shredded, draped and folded, looked for all the world like a huge figure dressed in rags just starting out on the arduous task of climbing up into the sky.

James was scared of the big plastic giant but he didn't tell no one about it, not even Olivia, not even when the wind blew and rattled that giant man's bones. J's Motto was MOUTH SHUT, his practice, in them days, was sticking to it.

#

Routine at the orphanage demanded a lot of getting used to and many lessons and concerts and debates. Boys and girls were kept separate and schooled in different ideas. The boys learned chemistry and French, the girls learned maths and displacement. There was no outward logic to it that anyone could guess but the rules were immovable.

J wrote a letter to his dad in condensation on the dormitory window, but the letters ran to bits and pieces like the letters in Hammer House Of Death.

#

The only chance for James and Olivia to be together was by participating in the out-of-normal-schooling-time dramatic 'entertainment' organazized by one of the most fearsome 'teachers' called Gormenghast.

G had written a complex long drama abt the life story of Madame Curie, a person from history who invented something called Radiations and later (apparently) died as a result. It was hard for J (or anyone) to understand what the point or message of this story was meant to imply. Girls in hoop skirts represented radium atoms, boys in black clothes painted white were a chorus of X-rays and the whole thing was broken up with nervous musical interludes of indeterminate length.

#

After audition O secured a small part in the play (probably as a wood-nymph) and she brought James along too, lending him a pair of her old brown tights to wear and covering their faces completely in that old brown make-up like the camouflage worn by DEAD SOLDIER.

Rehearsals were late at nite-time in a part of

the orphanage called a BASEMENT and each nite began with the sombre eating of an extra meal—a thick grey gruel that turned the stomach shuddering. James looked once in his bowl and described it to Olivia, lip quivering with vivid repulsion—'just bits of a skeleton buried in mud'.

#

Gormenghast left a shadow wheresoever he walked (even in the dark) and was an object of great horror and speculation for many in the 'school'. After blocking one nite he stopped Olivia in the corridor and sternly drew her into a darkly lit and sweltering corner. Olivia gulped.

Gormenghast asked: "If she and James might take on the special responsibility of 'lighting' in the big production?"

He showed her the equipment, the many lanterns, the thick red velvet drapes eaten by 'moths' ©, the dusty vertiginous metal walkways looking down upon the stage and soon she was in love.

#

Rehearsals came and went and O spent many many hours perched high up looking down on the action of the stage, J sat beside her, while all the other unfortunate children came and went below like so many ants at the direction of the depressive Gormenghast.

"What is the play about?"

James asking Olivia. No sense of it in his head, the architecture too vast.

O: "It is not about something" she says. "It is something..."

An answer J could not understand. After the last scene ended he looked at his sister and smiled——teeth bad, heart good. O kissed him 'tenderly' and 'tears came in the eyes' ©. After weeks of absence enforced by the orphanage regime the time they spent together in rehearsals was valuable (and strange), just like when you see a dead friend in a dream and are so glad to meet them again.

#

November. A timetable crammed with extra rehearsals. The winter nites were 'long and deep' © and the wind told stories that no one wanted to hear.

DEAD SOLDIER himself lay many nites fox-holed in a box under James' dormitory bed, his eyes nightvision © but nothing to see, hidden and sobbing and neglected, lonelier by day and by night. Even when he was around, J was too frightened to remove him lest some other child should want him badly or steal him away.

All night DEAD SOLDIER was groaning and his 'body' ® was aching and James was ignoring the sound. 3 months in the box. 3 months of dark solitary in realistic colours and, like some kidsclub experiment in language acquisition, DEAD SOLDIER's moaning turned slowly but surely into words. Listen:

"Spuuurrch"

"Speeerrnch"

"Speech"

No one there to witness it. Nightime. Magic in a shoe box.

#

What DEAD SOLDIER talked to himself about when he had got language:

1. The dark.

2. How cold he was.

3. His dead buddies.

4. The idea of an enemy.

5. The power of the 'human spirit' in overcoming loneliness.

But in time, with no one to talk to, DEAD SOLDIER's language simply faded, receded—from new words to broken words to no words and simply moaning once again. Full cycle of life, lived utterly alone. Strangled groaning in the dark.

#

Dormitory. Most kids sleeping. One (1) up and moving.

At midnight 13 November James woke up and heard DEAD SOLDIER groaning, getting 'louder and louder and louder' ©. He rose and snuck silent to put a blanket snugly over the box under his bed, just trying to cut down the noise.

"Be brave DEAD SOLDIER..." he whispered, "just be brave..."

Good simile: like some part of his own 'soul' © lay there beneath his bed, dying, dying, very slowly. Did not want no one to notice.

At rehearsals J asked O if DEAD SOLDIER was gonna pull through. She smiled but then she looked out the window and would not answer, just like Dad never would.

#

A jumble of hard work and bitter scenes passed. James worried, like his own bones aching, his own skin getting cold. Indeed preparations for performances of that play authored by Gormenghast (abt Mme Curie) became long and increasingly complex, stressing everyone—G desperate to perfect every minute detail before letting the public see his 'fine efforts' and turn him into a laughing stock. Each day seemed to require an addition of new scenes, special effects and dances and G was more and more anxious and inclined to bursts of depressive temper. On Monday he sent the cast of Hydrogen Atoms back to their dormitories in tears, and on Tuesday he re-wrote sixty three (63) entire scenes in order to excise FOREVER the part played by one poor unfortunate x-ray.

James and Olivia watched all from above. O

taking notes. Fixing lighting cues. J staring down
in the shadows, thinking, looking and listening
for 'shapes' ©.

#

December. Dark music (from the Gormenghast thing)
played in that orphanage thru all hours of day and
nite, its sound spilling thru the dormitories
making sleep impossible, bringing ghosts from the
old brick walls. Add that to the constant sounds
of crying, pipes bursting and not-so-very-distant
mortar attacks and the air itself became a
festival of sounds.

Then one night from under James' bed there came
a new sound instead of all the above and the
constant moaning of DEAD SOLDIER: i.e. a sound
called SILENCE. James arose reluctantly,
butterflies in stomach, and pulled off the blanket
from the box. Silence continued. J with his white
fingers shaking and his white skin trembling and
his blue eyes locked open wide.

There inside the cardboard coffin of the box
lay DEAD SOLDIER curled tite and naked, like a
fist in a womb. James touched him softly and
didn't find a response. DEAD SOLDIER blank and
rigid with betrayal, soiled in sweat, his medals
discarded, his uniform shredded off and torn.
Desperate.

James could not cry.

To look into the eyes of DEAD SOLDIER and to

see 'nothing' ©. To see his eyes still faintly tracking movements, too late, too late, to see an expression of Palitoy 'Despair' ©.

They buried DEAD SOLDIER without religious service in the rough ground at edge of the orphanage kitchen gardens. James drew a picture of a rose. Olivia brought a book and she read from the story of earth and of RAMBO, she read from the poetry of Yeltsin, Maxwell and Roche De Sandoz. James cried and she held his hand and it rained and she read from the epic poem *La Bionica/The Bionic Woman* by Keats and several times she read out the last and saddest verse, what every schoolgirl in Endland (sic) knows by heart:

If I ever need a cold shoulder to cry on
I'll know where to come.

#

On the day of the premiere all the orphans (incl. O and James) worked near to all of the nite to get things in a state of readiness. The big clock ticking a countdown. The whole thing shadowed by the death of DEAD SOLDIER.

O worked hard and J interrupted every now and then to ask her some question, some query about the difference between life and death. He asked her which is more alive, a stone or a lizard? He asked her where do wounds come from? He asked her where is the name of a thing?

But no understanding could bring DEAD SOLDIER back. J and O stayed in the theatre late, when rehearsals were over——J sat silent in the darkened auditorium and watching intently while Olivia 'let the lights on the stage fade out one by one' ©.

#

It is a well known fact that there are more snakes than ladders in the great game of life, but not even the 'teacher' Gormenghast was prepared for the big amount of slithering down a long thin reptile what he was about to do in his artistic career.

Indeed despite the inevitable setbacks of mounting a big dramatic production in a corrupt institution for destitute children and despite having to replace the original Mme Curie on account of unfortunate illness etc, Gormenghast was really thinking that his work was nearly done and all very well.

But G fell victim to his own 'flair' as is often the case with many of that caste and made some troublesome moments, eg his decision that for reasons of artistical veracity he ought to use real radium in the final sections of the play was a mistaken one even if it was a breakthrough in a certain kind of illegal theatrical realism. The audience were already in their seats when he began to pass out the faintly glowing yellow capsules using metal tongs in the gloom backstage and no one had the institutional or moral authority to stop him. From that moment on his fate was sealed.

James stood in the dark and practised the one line he still had to say as part of a chorus scene. "Half-life," he repeated. "Half-life, half-life."

Gormenghast's deep shadow. Curtain rising.

#

Act One. Very many of the cast became ill—complaining of headaches, dizziness and nausea even before the little radiation badges they wore began to change colour at an alarmingly fast rate of speed.

Act Two. That sudden feeling when life seems distant or unreal.

Act Three. The cast were soon severely depleted and several of the audience members were also rushing outside, retching technicolour. Coughing breaking out and fighting in the confusion.

A temporary caesura in the narrative while a medical officer attended to a few of the hydrogen atoms. The little ones dropping like flies. A plea for order. Chaos in the wings. Echoes of Zurich (1918) and The 100 Club. Outrage. Confusion. And the stench of death.

Gormenghast took the stage to remonstrate with the crowd.

It was at this moment, perched in their vantage point high among the walkways above the stage, that Olivia and James decided to take their chances and risk escaping rather than endure another season in the orphanage.

On the run

All the night and all the next morning James held O's hand by the motorway with the big wind rush as lorries thundered past, whipping the bitter dust and threatening to blow the children away.

First bloke took them to Leicester.

Second bloke took them to Hull.

Third bloke took them to Blackpool, or somewhere else in olde Endland (sic), or nearly near enough.

The lastest driver (thin and brittle) couldn't read, his eyes the colour of a week-old bruise, his manner slow like a ghost. There was something dangerous about him that both O and J recognised instantly—a man with bone hands and stickers of the Spice Girls spread all across the dash, a man adrift in signs he could not decipher. Somewhere past Grimthorp (sic) he gave O some paper, a folded scrap from deep inside his wallet, and asked her to read it to him.

She read—6 lines of sentimental verse. Doing 90 in the fast lane. Tears in eyes.

There was a kind of silence, after the reading, and in the silence James slept, his pretty head nodding, a frown across his face. O looked at the lorries and hoardings as they passed, wondering what (if anything) the driver must make of the slogans on the walls. A lorry went by, stacked high with cattle going somewhere to get burned. Another lorry passed, the back graffiti:

EVERYTHING IS FUCKED UP

and just below it, in a dry excitable hand:

GET READY.

#

J dreamt when dozing. It was him and Olivia—the 2 of them running, through rain and at night time again—the giant made from plastic rags abandoning his climb up the pylon and coming down to stalk right after James. A horror soundtrack, with breathing in the head and moonlight in the sky—like in the painting by Debussy: *'A Flight Across Astroturf Covered in "Dew"'*.

When James awoke he was sweating, his fingers knotted in the letters of his father's name.

#

Blue Boar Services or Leicester Forest East. A huge community mural showing the execution of Prince Charles. Guns. Flowers. Diana in the clouds.

When he dropped them, the thin man did not murder the children as they expected but rather he gave them money—for breakfast. J cried anyway in the sweet relief of incomprehension still shaken from the dream. In the services they ate hurriedly the standard fare of their world—a meal of chips, ketchup and mini-cheddars with a pudding of Spatsky's Chocolate Nooses.

#

At Blackpool they headed for the beach, walking hard on tired legs, past the FAIR & SQUARE CLUB and the Brick House, through the alley by the prison and from there to their old house.

O went to the door and knocked but J would not go on beyond the painted iron gate, preferring to watch his sister recede down the gravel path like a scene from some long forgotten 'film'. O knocked and knocked but there was no answer and only when her knuckles were red with human blood and when J joined her in the doorway, placing a hand upon her shoulder, did she stop. No neighbours to see them. All dead or gone away, their houses trashed or claimed by Bosnian Serbs.

The two of them walked round the back of the house (bungalow?) and Olivia forced a window, laughing at the noise and soon the two of them climbed inside. Like clambering back into the warmth and smell and close-to-nothingness of the womb.

#

The sun shone brightly in the garden beyond but days and weeks passed strangely in the old house as the 2 kids lived in there all alone. Every 'thing' held a memory, every smell a reminder, every corner a ghost. As empty and silent as it was, it seemed that the smallest of noises were magnified there, the tiniest of movements amplified—so that the crack sound of wood in the stairs or the strange heartbeat of the central heating could animate the whole space, populating it, scaring James and Olivia.

Of Dad and Harry there was no new sign. Just the traces of the life they had lived before the new days began.

When her own clothes got too dirty Olivia took to wearing her Mum's—a discarded shirt that shimmered like a strip cut out of the sea, a pair of old party shoes, with straps. Dressed like this she did the dishes, or spent long hours in front of the tv, watching ALL NEW FORECAST OF ASIAN MARKET CRASH and the rerun soap from Kasparov called ROBOT BEACH. Smoking Marlboro Lights. Drinking gin from the bottle in Dad's cupboard. Throwing books at the cats as they frolicked in the heat.

#

And while O drank, J stayed in the attic, marooned, immobile. He was busy with the task of shading his skin to stay just as pale and thin as ashes. He was busy with his pictures (Dad, Mum, Harry, a spaceship) and busy with the other great

75

task of trying 'to think of numbers that were bigger than possible':

"...two thousand million and hundreds of thousands and 62 thousand millions and one hundred and one dalmatians and ten millions and millions of gallons and 61 thousands of hundreds and millions of ninety three millions..."

He would list to Olivia before asking: "Is that bigger than possible?"

And Olivia would give no answer. Or some nights she would smile and say nothing, then blunder her pissed-up way to the bed.

#

Two visitors.

The first called DEAD SOLDIER. Back from the grave. Adept in real survival training, he arrived one dawn, crawling in thru the cat flap belly down, like under barbed wire, having dug himself out of the grave, his 'real gripping' fingers bloody with homing instinct, eyes swollen with travel and tiredness, his moaning turned to language once again.

There is a strange sight in the old house: James curled naked in his parents' old bed, himself the image of a foetus, the smaller foetus of DEAD SOLDIER cradled in his arms. A mix of shite white skin, moulded plastic, cold white sheets, sweat smell and earth. Gently the sun awoke them with its touch.

What DEAD SOLDIER talked to James all about:

1) The incredible journey.

2) Morality.

3) The futility of art.

4) His 'soul'.

5) New developments in warfare and technology.

Second visitor—Dad—arriving late one night. O and J didn't hear him enter, didn't hear him call.

But when they woke at lunchtime he was downstairs, waiting for them.

And things weren't very good.

Dad had a gun and he had pointed it at them.

#

Dad explained some things. How much of it was real and how much of it was not real was hard for either Olivia or James to understand. He was talking too quickly.

He explained about love, and where babies come from. He tried to explain the war which had left Endland (sic) in darkness. He explained that woman (in the sense of the feminine) is like a shadow— you chase her and she walks away, you run away and she follows. He explained about how a car engine works and how the operations of a human brain cannot correctly be compared to those of a computer. All this and other stuff he said he had learned in his long stay in a hospital for people whose heads or hearts have been broken into pieces (as he called it).

DEAD SOLDIER interrupted Dad's talking by moaning from upstairs. The shrill wretched sound continued, as hopeless as it ever had been and Dad went upstairs in a temper, took DEAD SOLDIER outside to the rockery and shot him twice in the face, a loud ricochet sending echoes in the street and a putrid stench of burned shattered 'plastic' hanging in the air for the rest of the afternoon.

Last of all Dad came back inside, shaking a little and poured himself a gin and stirred it with the gun and explained that Herod had issued a decree and that a census was to take place in Endland (sic). He said that everyone must return in haste forthwith to the town of their conception and there to be registered by full and legal statute of the law.
James cried.

Dad waved the gun he held in his hand a little, for emphasis. Olivia packed bags.

#

In the back of the car the kids could not talk openly but rather only mouth some rare words to each other, hoping that Dad would not catch sight of them in the rear view mirror. One time O wrote a note to J and she slipped it to him when they skidded round a corner and she smiled a bit and the note said HOPE but she dared not sign her name.

Dad talked all the time, like someone had cut out the valve between the tongue and the brain, his words a stream of signals, a tv jammed, a sickness of voice. He said the cuntry (sic) was all fucked up, he said the cuntry (sic) was going down (on someone ha ha), he said the planes were empty, the hotels were deserted, and the good spirits were staying away (all except for vodka). He said the olde cuntry (sic) needed a good olde fucking and he laughed like he made a joke that no one else in the car could understand.

Doncaster. Rotherham. Tirana. New Antwerpen. As they drove the roads were awash with travellers, caravans, great hordes, and persons going back to the source, thousands (1000s) of people heading in all directions. Many in cars and more still on foot, others in caravans of motorbikes, horses, oxen, even donkeys. All going back to the place of their conceptions. A thick tide of human persons and a flood of colours, ages, races, genders, sexes, types, shoe-sizes and ontologies, all pressed bumper to bumper. Broken cars at the roadside, great campfires on the edges of towns, the feeling of a country in distortion of itself.

And at the centre of it somehow Dad. Talking and talking. Like the cuntry (sic) was him, or he felt it was him. Some confusion between him and it (the cuntry). Some confusion of the borders.

#

And of all the talking he heard, James only really remembered one thing. One thing that truly scared him, one thing that cut him, one thing (1) that kept him awake that nite when they lay in the car, lit by moonfall, covered up in a blanket and trying to find sleep in the forecourt of a burned out DIY Superstore called DO IT RIGHT.

Dad said: "Do you hear me? You hear me alright?"

Olivia said: "Yes, we hear you..."

And Dad said: "When everyone gets back in the town of their conception(s) I tell yer something, I tell yer..."

"What?" James asked him, getting tired of the bullshit.

"I tell you that would be a perfect time for the universe to end..."

Dad laughed. He called the census a psychic equalisation, a millennial balancing of books. He laughed and called it Herod's joke. A counting up. A chance to get back to where time really started. A chance to have his kids (and all others) sleep again (for one last time) in the bed where they were made.

#

In the morning they set off again going many leagues to the westerly direction and within a day or two they caught sight of their destination— the city of C____ in the province of D_____ where

80

men call each other 'brother' and where the women are dark haired, long legged and free.

Dad slammed car doors and walked into the Hotel De Ville, demanding room 236 and leading the kids up there in confidence. It was a small room, just like he remembered, closed tight on a double bed, with shit brown curtains and a picture on the wall that caught James' eye.

Dad broke open the mini-bar and reluctantly shared a vodka bottle with Olivia while James stared at the picture, stood up on the bed in his muddy shoes, but no one really cared.

The picture: one of those allegories popular in former times. Service Stations Of The Cross. Baroque detail. A masterpiece of luminescent highlighter pens. Christ on The Forecourt. Crucified. The gay centurions. Posh Spice at Christ's feet, wailing and weeping and washing diesel off of him with her long black hair. In the background Peter, Paul & Mary. A pair of winged pump attendants hovering in the air and sporting the fluttering banner in typical period style:
LORD FORGIVE THEM THEY KNOW NOT WHAT THEY MOBIL.

James stared at the picture and an hour passed in an instant and it seemed to him so real he could smell the sand, and feel the breeze in Peter's hair.

#

It was only Mum's arrival that broke the spell. Dad and Olivia were both fast asleeping by then and James could not quite look at her or respond to her warm embrace.

Mum looked so different and the same and she had Harry with her. Harry was bigger and he didn't cry so much and his eyes followed you in the room and he smiled sometimes and James was happy to see him again.

Mum touched James' hair, touched his shoulder. She whispered him a few things—how she had missed him, how she loved him. She smelled of perfume and of some time that was a long time ago.

For a while James thought it might all be alright. He could look from Mum to Dad and Olivia where they had passed out on the bed and, even when the tv ran out of money and neither he nor Mum had more to put in the meter, he was happy, secretly, inside.

#

The only problem was that Dad would not sleep forever and, when he woke, then the shit really started. He hadn't seen Mum in 6 months but when he did see her—up close, in the same room and personal—he was not exactly overjoyed, even if she had brought Harry which fitted in with his 'plan'.

Dad was waving the gun and pacing the room. He wanted everyone to lie on the bed—the bed where

the kids were made he kept saying—everyone had
to lie down he said, it was a part of the census
(everyone right back where they came from) but it
didn't make much sense cos he wouldn't lie down
and he was making Mum nervous. She had blonde
hair, the colour of a girl's, and James could see
her eyes working overtime, trying to fix on Dad,
on the gun, on Harry crawling, on the slow
drawling movements which Olivia was making in no
particular relation to anything.

Up above their room people seemed to be moving
furniture all night—like the sound of thunder
thru the floorboards. Dad was talking loud. The
phone rang—Dad shot it. No way to know who it
was. Then Dad was talking, talking again. About
what he called right and wrong, about the
difference between action and inaction. About
magic.

And in the end Mum was talking too, only her
shit was less complicated. Just a lot of please,
please, please, and a lot of can't we just this
and can't we just that. A lot of old shit came
up. And some new shit. But the words didn't mean
much to James—it was more like a great angry
song, very strong, very long.

At some point Mum got up and started
gesticulations—a strange dance to go with the
long song and then Dad shot her, just like he shot
DEAD SOLDIER. And she moved a lot and then after
a time she was very very still and then Dad shot

Harry and he was trying to shoot James but he missed and he shot Olivia by accident expect he probably would've shot her anyway in the end.

Dad laughed a bit and said 'same price anyhow'. James crawled under the bed and crawled and crawled and started to cry. Didn't know what else to do. He could hear the rain start up again outside. He tried to think what DEAD SOLDIER had told him once, what seemed like an eternity ago, about something he didn't quite understand, about something DEAD SOLDIER called 'the futility of art' and it seemed to James that this knowledge more than any other might be of some use to him then.

James sobbed and while he sobbed Dad's arms came groping under the bed with the gun in the fist, a big dark eye looking for him, a big blind snake worrying for heat.

James muttered to himself what he could remember of DEAD SOLDIER'S thesis, tumbling it out from under his breath between sobs: "art is futile because... because it can't transform the material circumstances of a soldier or a worker or a whore... art is futile because it cannot change the world, art is futile because it cannot change the world."

#

Midnight chimed.

And then James stopped silent in his talking,

froze still and just quiet as ice. Dad's hand was coming towards him across a carpet and if you stared at the carpet close up you could see it bore those strange repeating patterns of dead leaves and faces drowned in brackish water that were popular some years ago. All was slow and quiet under the bed where James was made. And in the quiet of slow time James stopped his sobs and spoke again.

He asked:

"Who can sing a song to un-frighten me?"

And when he asked that the gun hand stopped snaking for a moment. Paused, in recognition.

And he asked it again. The stink of vinyl mattress. A voice from under the bed. From where he lay there thru the gap J could see the whole world framed like in peering thru a letterbox. He could see Mum's feet and legs, all crossed at an awkward angle and he could see a pool of blood slowly collecting in a lazy eddy by the chipped formica bedside unit, which (the blood) he supposed to be coming from Olivia. He knew then they both were dead and Harry too.

"Who can sing a song to un-frighten me?"

#

James lay still and watched the gun hand withdraw, blank, repentant. And he lay silently under the bed. Face pressed right to the carpet. And after a time of absolute silence he heard his Dad move a little and begin to sing. A soft slow reluctant song at first with words he couldn't hear. And the song got louder after a time. And the words a little clearer. The song: *Serenity.* What they call a 'traditional' song, whose many 'authors' were probably long legally deceased and all copyright long since long expired.

Something about love. Something about loss. About desire. And again about desire.

And somewhere in it, like some statutory requirement, a single little line about hope.

And then James heard his dad sit down on the plastic/wicker chair and he heard the gun click and then he heard the gun fire.

The shot like thunder. Then silence. No more singing. And then he knew it was over.

#

Only when the singing was over, in the silence that follows a great gunshot, was it clear to James that the tv was still on. Its voices chattering.

He lay under the bed many hours and watched the light in the room shift from blue to black to red and yellow and then to clear again. The tv flickering through cycles—news, adverts, a drama, adverts, updates on the chaos of the census, adverts again. And sometime deep in the night/morning there was a science programme. A tv voice that spoke of suns and stars and radiation.

A soothing, dreaming tv voice. Dawn came and James dozed in the crawl space under the bed where he was made. Asleep in a room full of corpses.

Objects recovered from memory. A last dream of DEAD SOLDIER and of lost KANGAROO. Like saying goodbye.

In the garden, back in C_____, DEAD SOLDIER collects his pieces from the rockery and surrounding flower beds, finding broken bloody plastic and bones. He reassembles, fixing himself with an eerie, methodical calm and then he walks the roadsides, the riverbeds and the shopping malls until he finds KANGAROO somewhere and in the 'muted desolation' © of the dream he leads again a quest, but not to find James this time. Instead he leads a quest to find the factory of his making, the place of conception for him and KANGAROO, a return to the source. In the dream they are adrift in the landscape of Endland (sic) and looking without map, compass or certainty for the city called 'Korea'. The strange camaraderie of ignorance, beauty and the road.

The tv news talked about the census. There were pictures from all across the world.

James dreamed a rag thrown to the ground, turning into a flock of ravens swooping over the ground. He dreamed a racing shadow turning into a running dog, a face that dissolved into rain. He dreamed. He shook beneath the bed.

In his dream he turned into glass and shattered

and in the corner of his vision there were a little display of his lives—the red lights telling him how much of strength he had left, how much of bullets he had left, how much of love he had left over all and the lights were blinking, flickering red to deepest black.

Low on energy, low on lives and low on love. Not much of anything left. Fading.

#

Morning came and James awoke regardless of the bad dreaming from the night. Crawling out on his belly from under the bed.

He kissed Olivia, Mum and Harry where they lay. He looked at Dad for a long time but somehow could not kiss him and he remembered Dad at the nite picnic where the strange glow of the headlamps had reflected on the blanket to make his tears look just like a Premonition of Blood.

James used his little fingers to close his dad's tired eyes. And then he left alone, 'to see what it was that could be done' © upon the earth.

#

Listen. Final cue.

LX 98. A fade out. Kid walking.

Sheffield.

The whole fucking world is morphing tonight sweetheart, a dark dark night, a dark dark night in Endland (sic).

The Shell Garages
History Of Mud

Melanie lived near the park and when she reached puberty at age unlucky 13 she was often sneaking boys over the railings at nite and across the dark green grass and into the bouncy castle.

What they did in there is no one else's business, but locals were often disturbed and complaining abt all sounds of sexual intercourse and stench of cider coming from the plastic portcullis doorway and even from a great distance (100m) you could see the turrets bouncing (hard) by moonlight at midnight.

#

All this happened before the famine.

Mel's dad was a stupid intolerant cunt—that sort of bloke what spits on the ground for emphasis in a conversation, belches and only reads on the toilet. Anyway. When the general scandal abt Melanie reached big proportions on the estate, he had 'words' with her and then 'more words' and then in the end 'a lot of words' ©.

He told her the law concerning young people and the law concerning wrong people and the power of the state in what he termed late late capitalism. Mellers shrugged and moved out the house for a few days. Then she moved back in again.

When the famine came, all hell broke loose in Endland (sic)—some blokes from the Council went round writing HUNGER in the walls and Olde McDonalds closed down and the place were like a dump of olden times where people died of cholera, raisins, mumps, vertigo and Russian Mattress.

#

Mel and her dad took to eating at nite, since local tradition dictated they had to give food to anyone arriving at mealtimes, and in this clever way they (like many others) lived lonely and bitter thru the famine and survived. Indeed a strange nocturnal culture grew up in their town (or so people sed) where people scavenged all day and then ate like ghosts at nitetime, windows lit a dirty Osram 40w orange in the dark.

Who gives a fuck?

#

Of course it dint take Mel long to work out a connection between sex and economics, and thereafter her visits to the park and bouncy castle resumed. Mel took the town's chief of police into the bouncy castle (20 mins) and she took N******* W********* the corrupt local govt official from Land and Planning (43 mins) and loads of other persons too (on a average of 21 mins per person).

In this way Mel and her dad did not want no more for food no matter abt the state of the nation what twats were always talking about it and writing various plays. They were all right Jacko and had Trebor mints and oven chips, chocolate

eggs, juleps and Krazy Glue for omelettes and each
alternate Sunday they had a whole chicken cooked
factory-farmer style in Giant Diet Lilt.

Such were the days they called their 'delicacy
days' ©.

#

One bloke that took a fancy to Mellers and liked
to bounce her pretty often in the castle was
called Vortex; a man 2-thirds human and 1-third
god. In fact according to many people he was also
3-thirds dickhead as well, but that is by the by.
Anyway Vortex was down at earth on a spell of
banishment following a minor indiscretion he'd
had with *********** the thin blonde German girl
whose name no one could remember and who Zeus was
nobbing.

Vortex used to talk to Mellers in proper Roman
English and kissed her with his tongue.

#

When Mellers was 21 she announced it to Vortex
that she really wanted to leave her dad and be
reunited with her mum who still lived on the other
side of the world in 'Iceland' or 'Freezer World'
or whatever.

Mellers and Vortex went to a party that had a
fight, a break-up and people snogging in the
toilet. While he was drunk Vortex sed he'd help
Mellers get the airfare together to visit 'Freezer

World', but instead when sober he dipped into her savings and skipped off to Berlin to see a mate of his who was working as a site foreman at some of the recent building works at Potsdamn Platz.

Like the poets say 'our private lives quite often get rewritten' by the fallout of historical events happening hundreds (100s) even thousands (1,000s) of miles away.

#

With Vortex (and her savings) gone, Mellers became depressed. She cried herself to sleep some nites and stared herself out in the mirror some days, high on a drug called Dunblane, skull full of bad bad dreams.

Ill luck followed ill luck. Her dad died in bungee-jumping accident, his house got bulldozed to make way for a by-pass and the bouncy castle got deflated as winter approached, a stain of dank looking grass beneath it providing the only 'poignant reminder' © of where the joys and great screws of her life had once been conducted.

#

Mellers began to collect books, esp the free ones you sometimes get at petrol stations. She liked PERPA-TRAITOR MONTHLY and another one called GOD'S BIG & LARGE WORLD OF NATURE but her fave of all was the SHELL GARAGES HISTORY OF MUD (part 1 in a series of 8). She loved the pictures in it and the words too, the sexplanations of what mud actually is, why we need it, how it helps make the world a better place and stuff like that.

A local dignitary took pity on Mellers and allowed her to move into his house. He lived out twds Santa Monica (so not really in La La Land at all) but he was still a decent sort who remembered 'life before the curfew'.

#

Life with the dignitary took some getting used to.

He had a car and a swimming pool. He had a gun and a telescope. He had a patio and two Japanese kids by a previous marriage, what Mellers ended up looking after while he was in various meetings about his parole.

The 2 kids (one 12 and one 16) spoke a kind of street Japanese that was a long way from the business class jap-crap that Mellers had learned back at school. Anyhow, it was all exhausting and one night (after putting the kids to bed) Mellers fell into a dozy sleep on the couch. Imagine this—the tv was on, playing one of those olde shows that 'everyone' loves and the patio door was open, a faint breeze stirring the windmills of her mind (?)... weird music played...

#

As Mellers slept so sweetly the Gods in 'Heaven' looked down and saw her and cried. Leia, Thor,

Hand-Job, Trumpton and Asparagus took pity on her and sent down their winged messenger called Dumbo.

"Fear not" sed Dumbo, when Mellers woke up in a mighty dread, "I am here to help you," or so the legend goes.

Mellers was 'all scared' but soon adjusted to what was happening and even turned the tv down so she could hear properly. Dumbo lent Mellers magic wings so she could fly across the world, visiting her mother and wreaking vengeance on Vortex.

#

First port of call:

In 'Freezer World' Mellers stayed a long time with her mum, learning the old ways and sitting by the camping gaz campfire till dawn, singing songs and doing the actions that go with them.

Mellers and Leia in the woods, laughing, stalking 'real deer' ©.

Mellers learning ITV magic, a book by Penn and Teller in one hand and a corpse of a rabbit in the other.

Mellers in a pub in Helsinki, telling jokes and falling drunk to the floor, dreaming of the Gods again, walking hand in hand with them and all crap like that.

#

Second (and ultimate) port of call:

Mellers comes flying into Vortex's new place in

Berlin sporting Dumbo's wings and a hammer what she's borrowed from Thor.

SMASH! goes his skull. KERRASSHHHH! goes his knees. KERR-SNAP! goes his neck.

SHHHCCLUUP! goes his eyes popping out of his 'head'.

Ha, ha, ha, ha! goes Mellers and all the Gods in Heaven.

#

Mud is a good and necessary thing. It makes the gutters be what they are and the basements of old buildings more interesting. Without mud the world would be an emptier and less enjoyable place.

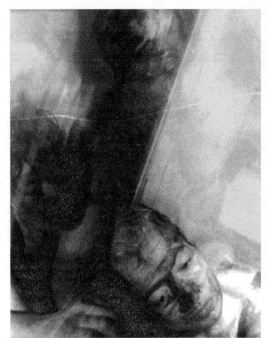

Kelly

Kelly's dad had an apple to stand in for his patience, and if she or 1 (one) of her many naughty brothers broke 1 (one) of the rules he would take a bite from that apple and simply swallow it, repressing his anger and right to retribution, saying nothing and 'staying his hand' ©.

In this way days, weeks or even a occasional month could pass without a beating at 473 New Garden Terrace in Endland (sic), and just the sight of a dwindling yellow apple to keep a child awake or on its toes.

#

Days of tension, brite nites of dreams.

Kelly's father had a stonemason come round their flat and carve in the words UTOPIA on the doorstep but she dint think he meant it literally—just as an indication of what he and his family were striving for and regardless what filth the other scum on the estate decided to chase after.

Only when the last bite of his apple was done would Kelly's father strike—instantly scalding that child unlucky enough to have 'finished the fruit' (as he termed it) and sending it down to FAST FOOD to get another one (an apple) before administering actual bodily punishment of a grievous/hideous kind.

#

That there were possible abuses to this system is so fucking obvious as it is also inevitable that in any society the weak will sink and the strong will rise and that there will emerge a type or class what manipulate the apparatus of justice and the law and 'prosper in every event' ©.

Kelly, for her part, was one of the sinkers and in fact, to extend out our metaphor, she was just that kind of weight some persons might use to put inside a sports bag full of unfortunate other animals and cause them all to drown.

#

Kelly lacked guile. She did not limit her misbehaviour to the time when an apple was fresh and therefore unlikely to be 'finished' but rather sinned willy nilly and thus very often 'finished the fruit'.

Kelly was dumb. When sent to purchase another apple from FAST FOOD she did not look round for a bloody great big one (like what her brothers did) but bought some cheap and poxy thing that her dad could finish off easy in less than 5 bites.

Kelly got some poisons. She put them in her father's apple and killed him, really slowly, really painful, really bad.

#

Revenged in this way Kelly left home and moved to Corsica. She got off with a bloke, the son of a foreign dictator (or so he said) whose father had been shot and hanged at a roundabout. Kelly wanted to know everything abt this new man—all abt his country, all abt his language, all abt his dreams, and all abt his father—was he hanged to death in the street and then shot repeatedly for target practice or was he shot in private and then just hanged up at the roundabout to be put on display?

Alphonse (the bloke) was a trivial person and he dint like the way Kelly dwelt on suchlike direness and destruction. Her biro doodles (of wars, massacres and perverted tortures etc) that she always did on the little jotter by the telephone upset him and within a year (one year) he was threatening to leave.

#

Round this time it was Xmas in Endland (sic) and Alphonse got a job at a olde fashionde Dept Store playing Father Xmas in a grotto of snow-land and freezer cabinets provided by Zanussi and Zyklon. Some nites when he came in he was still blue with the cold and shaken by the strange requests many kids whispered to him when out of earshot of their parents or legal guardians.

Alphonse would sit in front of the TV at home and watch his fave programme called DOCTOR OF MEAT. When the doctor of the title performed a tense and difficult operation, Alphonse took one swig of Vodka; when the doctor of the title kissed a sexually attractive nurse, Alphonse took two swigs of Vodka; and when the doctor of the title said his catchphrase "Look out for me in the scrub-up my friend", Alphonse took two swigs of vodka, removed an item of clothing and then took two swigs of gin. When Marriane Pubis (the female lead in DOCTOR OF MEAT) came in boasting of some new husband/lover, Alphonse removed another item of clothes and drank a shot of a new drink called PERUVIA, by the same people what made SYPHILIS.

By the end of most evenings Alphonse was drunk on the sofa (couch) and naked by 9pm, his underpants swinging from the lightbulb in the centre of the room and a bottle of PERUVIA spilled on the floor. Poor Kelly.

#

Kelly tried to make Alphonse love her the only way she knew how—with money—but no matter how much she gave him it dint do no good. Alphonse's Xmas job as Father Xmas came to an end abruptly on Dec 23rd and Kelly was back in the driving seat of their relationship. She got work in a shop selling clothes to fat women. All day long fat women came in the shop and Kelly had to squeeze them into the garments and praise how they looked (etc).

Anyway.

With money saved up from Kelly's job (with the fat women), Alphonse and Kelly decided to go on holiday as a way of sorting out their relationship. They went to a coastal town in a military resort called FORT FOG near Blackpool.

Arrival in FORT FOG was difficult because the fog was so bad. The travelling caravan (or coach?) what they were in had to stop on the outskirts of town and all the refugees got off and wandered around all lost, blundering, bags of belongings on their backs. There was a terrible argument over who exactly had won the sweepstake abt how many miles it was from Blackburn to this new place, but this ugly incident got forgotten pretty quick when the rain started.

Alphonse and Kelly found their hotel and kipped down for the night but trying to sleep at all was truly like a bad movie full of feel-sick moments. There were cries of agony and ecstasy in the street, the sound of gunshots in a far-off garden and at 3am someone burst into their room and threw a biscuit tin full of exploding fireworks onto the bed.

The holiday camp was run by cruel guards whose indifference to suffering was matched only by their insensitivity to joy.

#

In adversity (see above) the relationship between Kelly and Alphonse prospered again and their sex life was good. They had oral sex, lips swollen with the heat and mouths watering, they had 'quick and unexpected sex' © including of ripped clothes and laughter, they had violent and degrading sex in the case of which pain and its opposite were intertwined, they had pseudo-mystical type sex in which the sense of individual was lost to a sense of joint body—sweated, exhausted and lost. Sometimes even, late, late, late at night they had sex in the visionary position—sat apart and opposite on far sides of the room with the light on, staring at each other and masturbating in a mixture of fear, delight, hatred and desire.

#

The package week in FORT FOG came to an end and Kelly and Alphonse had to pack again and go. Everything seemed to be going OK but then there was some trouble at the airport and in the end it turned out Kelly had the right papers to leave and Alphonse did not.

It was one of those awkward moments that always happen at Customs/Immigration but Kelly knew she had no real choice—indeed it was either abandon Alphonse, get on the plane and live or else stay and face a life of boredom and uncertainty in a foreign hotel.

Kelly kissed A for the last time and got on the plane. As it lifted off from the Embassy roof Alphonse and the others were still clinging to those kind of skiddy bits on the bottom of the helicopter.

#

Back home Kelly drifted. She visited her dad's grave and spit on it. She went into town and came across a march where some people were protesting against the Job Seekers Allowance (JSA). Without really thinking Kelly joined in and later got arrested.

She came to a field where some soldiers were playing football with a human head. She sat on the touchline idly, watching and trying to keep up with the score.

It seemed to Kelly like her whole life were like some kind of dream.

#

One night a month (1 month) later Kelly got a call from her sister Elaine of whom she had not heard so much as a fuckin peep for several years. After terse (short) conversation they agreed to meet in town next day at the dysfunctional fountain in the old new shopping centre (the one they built before they built the other one).

The fountain, when K found it, was still with some water in it and a scum of bubbles and a few coins in there too. Kelly stood for ages and waited, watching a couple of black kids trying to fish the coins out with a bent coat hanger and a dirty polythene bag for a net.

Elaine was barely recognisable when she showed up, having gained 6 or seven stone after the bust-up of her marriage to a Turkish migrant worker. "I have ballooned..." sed Elaine, by way of dumb and unnecessary explanation.

#

At first the conversation in a nearby Gin Palace was all trivia of which there is no need to report—the usual crap about telly, the weather, food, periods and the occult what women talk abt when they are alone. But then K and E turned their thoughts to the past and began to wonder abt their father.

"Did you kill him?" asked E.

"Yes" sed K.

"I'm glad" sed E. "How come you never told us?"

"I never thought anyone would understand."

"Maybe not. But I am glad you did it."

After lunch K said goodbye to E and went back to the fountain where the black kids were still fishing in the spewy water. E stood awhile and, like the poets say 'weighed up the weight of life' before offering to help them, her longer reach allowing her to scoop up several coins what had previously evaded the grasp of the outcasts.

#

Two dreams.

K dreams a fish wrapped in plastic.

Later the same night she dreams a horse tangled in barbed wire.

Strange to think that all animals are now extinct except man. And yet they apparently persist in Kelly's dreams, in some tortured form at least.

#

Kelly goes to the cinema to see a film called DARK HOUSE (X).

The plot is complex, betraying more the diverse and contradictory sensibilities of its overlarge group of screenwriters than it does of the characters and their motivations, at least if you believe what Baz Norman says in his write-up.

Only half way thru the film does Kelly realise it is set in FORT FOG and the apartment in it is in fact the one she once shared with Alphonse (see above).

Strange to see the bed what she and A had fucked in shared now by Sir Peter Violence and Carla Labia, stranger still to see Ludger Shat hovering on the stairs just outside in the dark, his trousers half down as if waiting for Labia, but also, of course, as if waiting for her.

#

After the film Kelly goes walking round the precinct and finds a bloke who will sell her drugs. She gets this stuff that when you shoot it up breaks the past into thousands of pieces then speeds it all up to replay.

Kelly checks into the Station Hotel and then, lying on the bed, staring upwards, she shoots up the stuff. Above her Kelly can see the decorative carved figures of rabbits and foxes curled amongst leaves in the plasterwork high on the early 20th century ceiling but the ceiling has been painted so many times with emulsion that the animals are somehow blurry, lost and twisted like her dreams.

#

Time shatters, speeds around.

K sees her dad again and talks to him.

She sees Alphonse again. And touches his dick.

Then she returns to some scene she has long forgotten and which in Sigmund Freudian terms is the origin of all her anxiety (etc etc). The scene is vivid but the contents tedious to all but her. She cannot confront it. She screams, runs into the bathroom (en suite) to hide. Her screams are covered by the sound of the departing trains.

She remembers the graffiti outside her house in the Falls road: SENTIMENTAL SUBJECTS ON TELEVISION ARE AN EMOTIONAL WANK OFF.

She remembers the sight of blood.

And then she is falling, falling falling.

#

K falls for thirteen years. She falls and falls. Then finally she falls through a hole in the welfare safety net and she keeps on falling, going down down and downtown into a dark hole till she lands and breaks her back on some stones.

When she awakes she is inside a cave in which the people are all sat facing away from the entrance, transfixed by the shadows cast on the wall of events taking place just outside.

K goes over to this lot and tries to persuade them that what they are looking at is just shadows or a video projection of some type, just fleeting images of the real world and not the real world itself. But the cave dwellers argue with her, transfixed by the shadows, seduced by them and the more K tries to argue the less convinced she is of her sanity and soon she is getting confused abt which way she thinks is out.

Anyway.

K is 43 when she comes out of the cave.

#

She goes back to the Central Hotel. And back to the bathroom, ostensibly to get her stuff but really for something else like 'appointment with destiny' ©.

With the door locked and there in the hotel bathroom Kelly cuts her wrists to see if there are rings inside the human body like there are in those great great redwood trees in Movie America.

Kelly looking for the rings, looking to see how old she really is. But when she cuts there's only blood, bone and wires.

Like that scene in DARK HOUSE (X), where nothing real is really real.

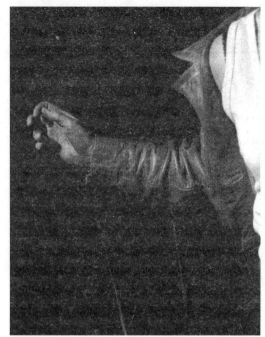

Morton &
Kermit

Morton's main problem was that he could not control his mouth. His brother Kermit was also a bit of a wanker. The town* where they both lived in Endland (sic) chanced to come beneath emergency military rule of the British Army and the two of them were soon executed by a firing squad.

*Liverpool

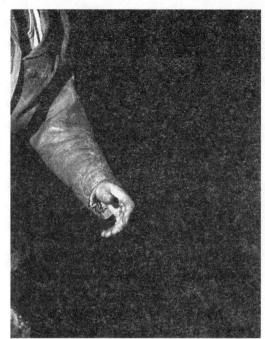

Crash Family
Robinson

Crash Family Robinson lived in a wood shack at the edge of town and heated water for their pot noodles etc on a stove. By day they chopped dumb wood, hunted 'slow bears' © and caught dead fish in the poison river. When there was time off from their chores, they went under the big bridge through the cold and onto Main Street to rent videos.

A picture of Crash Family Robinson shows them all in the half light. The youngest kids naked and suckling at their momma's tits, the elder ones playing with gameboys, the daughters washing up, with their hands in rubber gloves and Palmolive suds. Dad Robinson stands by the doorway to their cabin, looking proud. He is wearing a suit of sequins and carries in his hands a book to prove that he can read.

Meet the kids. There are nine of them in all —Ellen (1), Grace (3), Paul (5), Radioactive Boy (13), Blood Head (15), Particle Girl (17), Alistair (23), Violetta (21) and Shaun (25).

Some nights when the videos are finished and Dad Robinson has stopped his jackanory from whatever dumb-ass book he's reading, the teenagers sneak out the cabin and get up to their pranks.

Particle Girl makes nuisance calls to lonely women, waking them up, making their hearts tremble and their nights long. Blood Head walks by the canal brooding over the bodies that float there, and the gun-men, narcs and whores that haunt the tow paths. Radioactive Boy rearranges the stars in the sky over Manchester to say rude messages, terrorising the whole town. At least in their dreams.

At breakfast the teenagers are tired and ugly, rat-arsed with lack of sleep while the rest of the bairns are bright eyed and bushy tailed. Dad Robinson reads the newspaper aloud full of GEORGE DAVIES IS INNOCENT and KILL THE FUCKING PIGS, mom serves gruel from a big pan, a baby still stuck to each tit.

Of course the logging business aint what it used to be and to make up for it and keep the family afloat Alistair, Violetta and Shaun dabble in the darker edges of politics. When they aren't chopping wood or larking around naked in a fucking waterfall they are scheming to make money and power in the city. Wire-taps, bribery, blackmail and corruption are a lifeblood to them and ma and pa don't know it any more than they suspect the 'midnight ramblings' etc of the teenagers.

One night (Nov 23rd) Violetta and Shaun slip off into town to pick up some dirt and bribe money for laundering in a car-park. Something goes wrong (a big plot device with like a double/triple cross and counter cross betrayal thing that'd take too long to explain) and they end up killing some guy in the shoot-out. The bloke what gets it is a minor govt official who's queer and in need of cash to pay for a holiday in Thailand.

Shaun, for his own efforts in the shootout, gets a bullet in the leg and he and Vi struggle to make it back to the wooden shack in a stolen car, deadman's blood on their shoes and a suitcase full of forged Danish Kroner in the boot.

As the car bumps into their driveway a cock crows three times and from this bad omen things only get worse. A sheep is born inside out and the Pac-Men on Alistair's Game-Boy go ape-shit suicidal, eating each other and hanging themselves on digital trees.

On the third night of bad omens etc the ghost of the queer bloke from the car park comes back to haunt them all, moaning and jangling his chains outside the windows of their shack so Dad Robinson in his sequinned suit can't help but wake up and ask what the fucking hell is going on. The ghost of the queer bloke sees him and flees, leaving a message written in Anti Freeze on the windows:

WATCH OUT ASSHOLE it says, and LEAH BETTS SPEAKS.

On its third visit the ghost of the queer bloke comes into the house. Pa wakes—gives him coffee and pie. The little ones stir, sleeping and dreaming of cot-death in their beds beneath the stairs. The ghost of the queer bloke finishes his coffee, delivers a dire warning (threatens yrs of plague dogs and Thatcherism), promises 'revenge revenge' in a shrill queer voice and leaves.

Pa can't sleep, can't get back to sleep. He tries counting sheep, stars, satellites, sirens, slaloms, skylarks, anything, but nothing gets him to sleep so in the end he hits the bottle. Picture this—Pa drinking bathtub gin from a free-with-petrol tumbler, hands shaking, the future of his family, his acre of land, the field where Gramps is buried etc etc all rolling thru his small mind.

By and by things happen for the worse. Ghost of the queer bloke from the carpark keeps coming back and back, repeating on them like bad curry from the Taj Mahal on High Street and freaking everyone out. The haunting drives them crazy and the land itself is poisoned too. Crops won't grow, river won't flow. All politics schemes of the kids go wrong, the Gods desert them, dead man brings disaster. Some bitch photographer called Dorothea Lange starts hanging round the shack, taking pictures. Before long the riverbed looks like crazy paving at Cromwell Street and ma's tits are dry too.

Come Springtime the whole family goes walking into town, not as astronaut Kennedy princes, but as paupers. They barefoot, they ragged. You can see their ribs and the people in the mall look at them funny cos they dressed so unfashionable. GAP don't sell that kind of thing anymore. Dumb clothes and wide empty smiles.

Crash Family Robinson end up living in an underpass. The kids beg. Ma drinks and Dad reads. He reads about HEAVEN and REDEMPTION, he reads about POLITICS. He reads anything he can.

Through the year of 39 the family die one by

one. Palsy, dropsy, plague, AIDS, clap, 2 murders and a suicide. The babes of course are taken into care—adoption fodder for rich non-whites overseas—never to be heard of again. Only Blood Head, of the others, survives—getting a job in a pub on the Manor Estate and acting as an unofficial bouncer in the bookies round the corner.

Days, years and months pass. Blood Head works hard, stays warm in the winters, gets stock in the bookies and invests it wisely. Before long he is head of the company—a monument to hard work. He marries, has kids of his own, gets a life. But no matter how much Bahamian Holidays and Rum Fucking Punch on his desk or fat cash in his wallet, there's a photo what shows the CRASH FAMILY ROBINSON all round their table in the outback, in happier times. Each day Blood Head still looks at that picture and each day he cries.

In the wings of history the ghost of the queer bloke from the car park laughs loudly and shuffles his chains muttering the old lie:

Dulce Et Decorum Est Pro Patria Mori.

Some kinds of dying take longer than others.

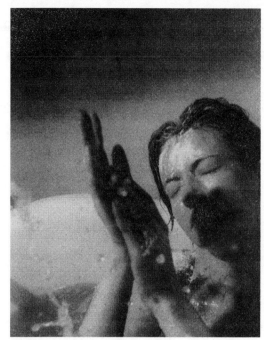

Wendy's Daughter

When Wendy went on tv's LOW BUDGET QUICK QUIZ the host Bob Peter asked her where she came from and Wendy told him, "Hell". Her words had a ring of truth abt them—the place she lived was near Doncaster (near junction 38) and various gangs had run long there and run loose too, breaking windows and stealing milk on the council estates.

Wendy never made it to the QUICK QUIZ play off (about which no-one was surprised) but she did get a QUICK QUIZ Mattress and a QUICK QUIZ Donkey Jacket and a QUICK QUIZ Libel Suit on account of how she'd broken the contractual requirement for lightness of tone at all times. Bob Peter told her straight up—some people make good tv and some don't—she was in the latter group.

From the day she fucked up on QUICK QUIZ Wendy wore a t-shirt saying OUT OF CONTROL and she couldn't sleep at night or keep her food down. The doctor said she was suffering from post-NATO depression but that didn't mean fuck-shit to Wendy or anyone else of her kind.

Wendy was a single mother and her little kids' Uncles were a large and indiscriminate throng. There was Bad Jensen and Torvald Hemmingden, there was Rudi Schropp-Pedersen and also the twins Chris and Stephen Arne Naamansen.

#

One night Wendy curled up tite in her bed with her daughter (whose name was Grief) and Wendy woke screaming from a dream. In the dream Bob Peter (host of QUICK QUIZ) was one of her best mates and they were hanging out together down at the mall and shoplifting, often stealing more than they needed to or things they didn't want. The security guards in the dream were getting confused because in the dream they were finding lots of half-eaten Chanel Chocolates and other things stuffed in the cisterns of the toilets in the dream.

Round this time Wendy was working in a crack factory or a cracker factory and she always brought stuff home with her so she and her daughter got plenty to eat even if it was a monotonous diet. They certainly had plenty of energy, or at least that's what the neighbours sed for they never stopped complaining abt the noize that they had to cum on and feel all the fucking time.

#

By and by things happened and Wendy's daughter (Grief) enrolled at night school to study old Sanskrit language and quantum math. She was a good student (not like her mum) and much could be learned from her as an example to other persons. She got good grades and even helped the other students with some of the mortally difficult tasks. One of the students was chained to a cliff-side and every night an eagle returned to eat his liver and each day when the sun came up the liver re-grew again and Grief brought the man a drink of water.

One week the teacher set Grief a question for homework, in fact a v. hard question of computational philosophy first posed by Mary Norum in her book FAT CHANCE: SOME PROBLEMS IN THE THEORY OF QUANTUM PARTICLE PATH PREDICTION (Sleep Press '96).

How the teacher laughed in his grey beard cos no one could answer Norum's question(s)—least of all a runty little night-school student. The best minds of many generations had been driven starving hysterical and naked by that Norum question(s) and not a one of them had solved it.

Grief started her homework on the bus back to the ghetto and when she got home she was already 'deep in thought' ©. Finding her mum asleep in front of the tv (watching NEW ADVENTURES OF ZEBRA-HEAD) and surrounded by old packets of crack (or crackers) she went straight upstairs and sat at her desk.

This was her big chance, she thought, to get some work done before her mum woke up and started playing Bloody Hell ®.

In the night's dark Grief studied the equations, rearranging them in her head and scratching at her scalp with the broke and bitten end of her biro. Down below her in the city there were the sound of some cop cars screaming to a rescue, and of some blind kids throwing stones at bottles and of some leaves falling from the advertisements for trees. It was autumn.

Grief sat there thinking hard and she got stiller and stiller in thought until in the end you could hardly see her breathing even so thoughtful was she and when Lars Frederick Klokkerfaldett (her latest Uncle) came banging on the door he could not wake her (or Wendy) or raise her or gain her attention or break her reverie or bring her to the door to let him in.

It was the Spring in fact when Grief awoke at last and a full six (6) months had passed since she first sat down at her desk, so deep in thought had she been. Her mum was dead on the couch of course and smelt real bad but the tv was still on and its bright Technicolor scenes filled the house with sounds and sickly sights.

Love is blind. Grief didn't cry but it wasn't for lack of sadness. She did not cry when the paramedics took her mum out of the house in polythene boxes and she did not cry at the funeral and she did not cry when Lars Frederick Klokkerfaldet came round for some books that he'd lent Wendy before she died.

Grief only cried a year later in fact, when she got drunk one night and got lost in a city called Copenhagen. Everybody has their own kind of mourning and Grief was no exception to this.

Only after the funeral and everything did Grief return to her homework and then she certainly did get a big surprise that would change her pathetic life for good.

Looking down at her notebooks you could see the tiny writing of her hands covering page after page after page and moving all the time clearly to a solution so neat and so simple—the solution that any scientist etc now knows as Grief's Solution —a fast scrawl of numbers and inspiration that bespoke the journey she had made whilst sitting at her window in strange and haunted trance. They say GOD or the Gods move in mysterious ways.

Of how Grief handed in her homework over 18 months late but still got a A+ from her teacher and how the rest of the world gave her an accolade and her peers in the sciences gave her a Nobel Prize and the Crack Co (Jacobs) gave her a pension on account of what happened to her mum, little need to be said here cos it's already the stuff of popular legend. Strange things happen in the history of the real world and although many times people despair of ever doing much in life or of finding their way, the story of Grief, daughter of Wendy that fucked up on QUICK QUIZ, is a inspiration to us all.

Grief is the patron saint of students and mathematicians and a poster of her kind face and pretty hands hangs to this day on the wall in every student union refectory, coffee-shop and bar.

V̶o̶i̶d̶House

or the sky still gets dark at night

Void House is the place where they shot the famous chase scenes for the end of BONE GRAFTERS II. If you look it up in Carmichael's Film Compendium you'll find it described as enjoying "a large and ill-deserved cult reputation". You'll read that the film is loved mainly by "critics with the eye, ear or stomach for unsavoury scenes". You'll hear that it is "a sub-standard sex film with a half-baked thriller sub-plot". There are running times, some talk of genre patterns and the vaguest intimations of the scandals surrounding this movie on-screen and off but no detail, no real facts, no effort to do justice at all.

Standing in the stairwells of VOID HOUSE now it's pretty hard to believe that once the likes of Carla Labia, Paunch Davies and George Van Genitals ran through them naked and smeared in gelignite. Hard to believe that director Ulrich Von Braun (brother of the rocket scientist) stood in consultation with cameraman Buzz Aldrin as they considered the innovations that would earn them a place in the history of exploitation cinema. Hard to believe (as one glances at the endless off-green corridors through the banal and nervous buzz of fluorescent lights) that this is the actual place with such a firm grip on the collective unconscious of our age, that these walls are the very walls that run with blood in so many nightmares turning adults into weeping children, that these doors are the doors that open on every travesty of human pleasure imaginable, that the fifth floor landing is the place which has inspired more terror and dread in the human heart than any other location this side of the death camps. And yet it is true. All true. And if the ghosts cannot be seen or felt always they can at least be named.

Carla Labia was 24 when she took the role of Marnie in BONE GRAFTERS II—she'd just broken up with her agent-cum-boyfriend Wagner Lasten and he asked her not to do the movie, told her not to do the movie, begged her not to do the movie but she went ahead and did it anyway, with the consequences so clear to everyone now.

Paunch Davies was at the end of the line (or in fact at the end of many many lines, mainly of cocaine what were supplied to him by his personal trainer/doctor and confidante Gruel Hampshire). After some false starts to his come-back career (a cameo in some tv shit and a sidekick role in the movie DOCTOR UNDER THE INFLUENCE) Davies was rolling back into the almost public arena with a series of unexpected porno flicks produced by Alfonso Verbatim—BONE GRAFTERS II was supposed to be just the latest of these, shot back-to-back with another project called UNDER THE SKIN. In the end, as shooting on BONE GRAFTERS took its almost inevitable turn towards extremity and excess, Davies was sacked from his other male lead in less than happy circumstances.

The rumour papers rumoured and the scandal papers scandalled, the Studio (VOSTOCK/RKO) made no comment and producer Verbatim merely said he was sorry to have to let such a good actor go. Those who knew would not speak on the record. But in private they whispered that the marks on Davies' back (the wounds, rope burns and other scars incurred making BONE GRAFTERS II) were creating irrevocable havoc for the make-up people on the parallel film. After a time, those that knew him said, it was more or less impossible to keep track of the damage let alone disguise it or check its progress on his body. Of the escalation of this process and its disastrous results we need say little here—it belongs rather later in our story.

#

Get a copy of BONE GRAFTERS II if you can. You'll see the deep dark stairwells of VOID HOUSE in the end credits sequence and the service tunnels and elevator shafts in its closing moments. As the end titles roll watch out for the name of Marriane Pubis—she went on to great things later altho it was only a cameo role for her. Her credit is as GIRL IN BAR but that's not really an adequate description of the look she gives Ludger Shat in the opening scene.

Anyhow. You should also check out the name of Quentin Collins when it goes by on the credits—he's listed a script editor but everyone knows he was just a boyfriend of the other male lead Andrej Kropotkin. And look out for Fillomena Petersen too—she was the continuity girl who had an on-set affair with the cameraman Buzz Aldrin. Petersen really had an eye for detail and her conscientiousness was legend on a set already steeped in that word.

Think about Petersen. If you stand in room 637 of VOID HOUSE you can still see some of the daubs of blood she placed high up on the ceiling—a spiral of spots and smearing fingerprints that had to be replaced seventeen times as the scene got re-shot in ever more complex and 'realistic' ways. Aldrin used to joke about Petersen, saying in some strangely affectionate way that she was really working for God: maintaining order, continuity and cohesion in a world that tended otherwise to flux and the incomprehensible.

It's fun to think of her maintaining order on the set of BONE GRAFTERS II. Dragging Sven Horblad out of the bathroom with the needle still stuck in his arm; trying to organise transport for the wounded extras; trying to find booze for Paunch Davies at 4AM when all the bars were closed; or even, as Aldrin described her, rearranging his apartment, removing her lipstick, her discarded underwear, the traces of ash from her cigarettes, making it seem for all the world like she never had been there. A continuity girl.

#

When they first released BONE GRAFTERS II there were scandals aplenty of course. It's true that the protests in Bible Belt Scotland, the riots in Sydney and the injuries on the West Bank could easily have been orchestrated by a decadent and cynical publicity department eager for press and attention. But not even Michael Verbige would have courted the deaths, the sixteen fatal heart attacks in less than six public previews of the film, or the attempt by George Van Genitals to take his name off the credits, or the suicide of so many minor role-players. Not even Verbige would have dared to contrive the tragic detainment (under the 1963 Mental Health Act, Section 23) of the chief scriptwriter Helena Tereshkova, or indeed the wider, broader effects of the movie on our collective unconscious to this day.

Given the events of March 1984, it's hard to be sure how much of the script Tereshkova really wrote. Her other work is incontestably mediocre —a string of adult comedy capers, standard loss-of-love-and-innocence movies and porno-chillers often set in the unremarkable town of Paris (Endland) where she grew up. If she did script it fully, BONE GRAFTERS II is really something of a U-turn, a creative breakthrough whose next logical step, we can only suppose, was the breakdown that claimed the life of her daughter (Joely, aged 5) in such regrettable circumstances and which cost Tereshkova her freedom and ultimately her mind.

If only one thing is certain now it is that Tereshkova herself will shed no light on the matter of the script. You can see her in the documentary BLINDED BY THE LIGHT (Vostock 1998) —a skinny birdlike creature in a secure wing of Rampton run by Virgin/Securicor, her eyes dull with medication, her attention permanently scrambled by the steady stream of ECT that has been the mainstay of her treatment in thirteen unlucky years, wrists scarred with the ploughed skin of so very many suicide attempts.

#

Those with a taste for literary analysis tend to put the script down to a three way combination—Tereshkova as the story framework and then Wilson and Callaghan as the real architects of the devil in the detail. The other writers credited—O'Neil, Evangelista O'Casey, and Moss—generally don't get much of a look-in on the scholarly attribution of lines and in any case it's well known that with actors like Paunch Davies and Ludger Shat on set, the chances of anyone sticking to the script were pretty remote.

People who've seen the facsimile working script of director Ulrich Von Braun (now lodged at the British Library) say that it's covered in blue-biro additions in the characteristic scrawl of Wilson. It's in Wilson's handwriting that the key lines for Marnie are written, in Wilson's handwriting that the scene people call the 'seventh circle of hell' has been written, in Wilson's handwriting that the sentence: 'no way out, no way out, no way out, no way out, no way out' is written repeatedly as the closing lines of the film.

Of the few persons who worked on the film still alive, still fewer are working in film anymore. For most VOID HOUSE was the final station of their own particular cross.

Paunch Davies died about three weeks before the first screening—a death caused by the build up of wounds inflicted during the filming itself. Copies of the autopsy are on the Internet pretty well everywhere. Check it out. The doctor says there's a limit to the amount of tissue a human body can regenerate—that Davies was well beyond acting, as well as well beyond reason in the final months of his life.

Von Braun never directed again and everyone knows what happened to Sven Horblad and Gruel Hampshire.

#

Take the stairs to the top of VOID HOUSE and take a look at the view. To the west you can see asphalt, acres of scorched concrete, deserted houses, teams clearing radioactive waste, a few remaining burned-out cars. You can hear the birds singing, you can see the stormclouds gather and disperse. There are those that find it hard to reconcile the place and the story of it—the facts and the fiction—the layerings of each. They say a film can cause bad dreams for an aeon, pulling the rug from under steady feet, sending shivers down so very many spines. It can send a culture into fear. But in the end it is only celluloid, so many column inches in so many industry rags. And when the fan club visits are over, when the photocalls and exorcisms are done, when the flowers on the little shrines are faded VOID HOUSE is just a building after all.

That's what people say sometimes but it isn't true.

If you walk to the East facing edge of the building and duck under the security fencing you can get to the place from which Carla Labia jumped and ended her short life the day after the premiere of the film in her home town of Bradford, Endland (sic). She was wearing the costume she wears at the start of BONE GRAFTERS II—the little red cocktail dress that the press agency people still seem to love so much. There wasn't a note. Just a list of the people she loved. And of her favourite places. And of her favourite journeys. And of her favourite books. There were rumours that she was several months pregnant—with a child conceived during filming itself. Take a look at her first big sex scene with Ludger Shat. People say that in its climactic moments there's a flash of recognition in her eyes as he comes deep inside her—that that's the moment when the child was conceived, a conception captured on celluloid, perhaps the only one in the whole history of cinema. It's possible, of course, like so many of these things, but none of it provable.

This spot on the roof facing East beyond the security grilles is really something of a pilgrimage place—a suicide spot (for young lovers and lone girls) so notorious now that it had round-the-clock security until recent cut-backs in local government spending. The pavement below has seen the final movements, murmurings and ecstasies of some several hundred people—most of them teenagers, many of them Japanese.

#

"The sky still gets dark at night..."

Those are Marnie's last words in BONE GRAFTERS II and those who found Carla's crumpled form on the ground below VOID HOUSE say she was whispering them then too.

"The sky still gets dark at night, the stars still shine, the earth still spins... these are the certainties we cling to, these are the certainties we cling to..."

On your way out take the elevator to the fifth floor landing and wait for the chilling so-familiar drone as it slows. Just close one eye and wait. As the door shudders open you can just about replicate the shot used by cameraman Aldrin to show the carnage in the second reel. Recall the bodies. The silence. The writing on the walls.

It's here on the fifth floor landing that those end words of Wilson's are still meant to appear on certain occasions and anniversaries, in certain light conditions, to certain people, written in shimmering blood.

A tv crew from Serbia came west one year and camped out outside the big dark building that is VOID HOUSE. They filmed the wall up there every day for a year and they never saw anything—going home to Sarajevo out of luck and over-budget, director destined for retirement. A scientist they hired took samples from the wall—he said he found traces of human blood and it was still fresh, much fresher than it should have been so many years after the event.

Ludger Shat said there was a feeling in the place, right from the very first day of the shoot, He said the air was cold. He said the silence was inhuman. He said you couldn't even dream safely in a place like that, let alone make fiction in it.

He makes a pilgrimage to the building every year or so. He leaves flowers on the paving slabs, says hello to some of the ageing extras who still live nearby and then gets back on the train to Glasgow with a bottle of whiskey and a packet of tranquillisers.

Ludger Shat still wears the promotional T-shirt he sported when making the film. It asks a simple question, made ironic by history:

BONE GRAFTERS II: WHAT HAPPENS WHEN SEX & DEATH GET CONFUSED?

And Ludger knows, if anyone does, but he's taking his secret to the grave.

Jonesy

Jonesey started taking niteclasses in a shite attempt to get the DHSS off his back. Each Friday he turned up down the old school where he used to go as a teenage arsehole and he went walking back in old glass classrooms and down smelly corridors of all memory lane (etc) to try and get his mind right. Jonesey got a tattoo that sed NOSTALGHIA on his forearm too. (Clever little cunt.)

That bloke what ran the jobclub arithmetic class only had one (1) arm and all girls thought he was 'definition of cool', giggling and blushing and fidgeting with their AIDS ribbons nervously whenever he came close. Jonesey sat at the back all time smirking and drawing doodles of lynchings and 'scenes of revulsion' ©. Weeks of maths, shorthand and history passed him by and (in shorthand) Jonesey got bored.

In week five the one-arm bloke got called up to the war which was happening abt this time and so was absent forever (since dead). The whole maths class was mortified and one of the girls in it got up and tried to say a few words of sweetness and remorse. Her name was Emma and her chair scraped on the tiles as she stood and there was a silence so great you could hear the woodlice in the skirting boards. Unfortunately Emma was one of those people who, everytime they say something even remotely poignant or sincere, a load of putrid music would swell up in the background and fuck the whole thing up. As the 1st words came out of her mouth people looked at her and were nearly moved but when the music came in they began to look shifty, looking away, even exiting the room. Jonesey never wept at all and couldn't give a shit—maths wasn't his strong suit anyhow.

#

In wake of bereavement old one-arm's class was disbanded and the pupils dispersed to other classes—the gigglers separated and confused, Jonesey himself sent off to some part of the school where he'd never been before. Passing up them concrete steps by the dried up lake Jonesey entered the entrance to a big new towerblock in the school, his dirty shoes leaving skid marks on linoleum tiles. What a strange thing time is thought Jonesey and what a strange thing is space...

Two hours later he was still reading all the class notices and directions of where he might go, confused by the new building and the flickering lites.

VOODOO ECONOMICS it sed in room B345.

SLEEPWALKING (Intermediate) it sed in room C69.

ORGANISED CRIME it sed in a different building called the H block.

Over weeks Jonesey took well to his new classes. He prospered in PALMISTRY & PREDICTION, he tried hard in TELEPATHY and knew no rivals in NIGHTMARES OF SUBTERFUGE. The bloke what ran that class called Jonesey a star pupil and the gigglers looked on him with new eyes and his quips from the back never failed to raise a smile.

Like the poets say 'love is a garden' or 'ignorance is bliss' and Jonesey was no exception to this. The girl that ran the class in AUTOSUGGESTION told him he should look in the mirror each morning and say "I like you, you're brilliant...", she told him he should whisper praise to his furniture, his telephone and his car. She told him that he should whisper 'good lies' to his kids as they slept and that when they awoke they would believe them.

Jonesey had no kids of course, but he whispered in the ears of anyone he caught sleeping and thanx to him (and God, Coolio, Aretha Franklin etc) these folks soon had photocopy memories, strong hearts and perfect vision. Niteschool was Jonesey's apotheosis and soon he knew all there was to know about the night. Indeed, in many ways he was the night, indistinguishable from it, cloaked, created and concealed in its power.

#

Weeks and months passed and Jonesey did well in life, eating chips from the chips van and poring by candlelight over interesting pamphlets like INSTRUCTIONS FOR DECEPTION. Only on the third day of the fourth month did things go wrong. Jonesey was just getting a bus into town to attend nightschool when someone further up in the queue collapsed from a broken heart. As a crowd of onlookers gathered Jonesey pushed his way through and attempted to revive the bloke. His attempt was successful and the bloke thanked him loads, local press (Shanghai Courier etc) showering him with photoflashes.

The attitude of the DHSS to this weren't too good though. So far as they were concerned Jonesey rescuing the bloke at the bus shelter was a kind of undeclared and hence illegal work. No matter that he received no remuneration from it or that a life was saved—Jonesey was a malingerer and hence not entitled to benefit henceforth. Worse than this, he was a law breaker and charged with 3 (three) separate counts of chequebook fraud and a further count of dancing naked in the woods with poppets and demons.

At the tribunal Jonesey was drunk on brandy but he kept remembering that advert for OFFICERS CHOICE whisky where it says in BIG letters: OFFICERS CHOICE WHISKY: *There's no choice...*

The jury were three men and nine women. Seven black, one Puerto Rican and four Anglos. The judge was a Chinese American and Jonesey got a dream-team of defence lawyers—many of them straight from Hollywood. As part of the defence strategy they dreamed up, Jonesey had to change his name but he found it hard to remember what his new names and many complex alibis were.

In prison, waiting for the trial to end,

Jonesey counted the days. He met up with a few of his old mates from nightschool or Borstal or whatever and they were soon up to their old tricks. Their favourite game was to astrally project out of the jail and go out on the town gambling and seducing women. Jonesey was good at this, so was Hank Marvin and Varmana Gupta. What a trio they made and what long conversations they had about the nature of real reality and how the guards never once noticed they were gone from their beds.

Anyway. Verdict day came surprisingly quick. Indeed after 11 months of evidence the jury reached its conclusion in a remarkable three hours of deliberation—Jonesey was innocent on all counts and released forthwith. Cheers in the courtroom and headlines bearing the name of Jonesey's pseudonym. J paid off his lawyers and quit while the going was good, heading down to Rapid City on a bus.

#

Rapid City did not earn its name from the amazing Rapids in the River there, but rather from the fact that time runs three times faster in that City than it does anywhere else. Jonesey went in and burned off a good few years. The pace is breakneck and draining on the body but for some at least the rewards are sufficient—for Jonesey it were 5 yrs of pleasure crammed into 1.7: no attachments, few consequences, no bother from the rest of the world. Rapid City was like the Foreign Legion for people that don't like fighting or discipline. A kind of Las Vegas on fast forward, leave your wristwatches at the door.

In truth Rapid City was more than pleasure though, for Jonesey came out of it changed—older, wiser, lean but still hungry (etc). And of course when Jonesey came out the true world had changed too. The airships no longer dropped bombs on London and Plymouth and the girls no longer wore Carling, Heineken or Skol. The nites were longer and the days were shorter and the world was 'more crueller' © too.

Jonesey needed to get back to Endland (sic) so he went down to that market and bought a donkey what had been painted by gypsies so it looked like a zebra. The gypsies wanted more money for the donkey on account of how it was supposed to be a zebra—"Look is rare, is rare animal: ZEB-RAH," the oldest gypo kept sayin and spelling out the name, black and white paint streaking off on his hands as he patted the beast. It took them 2 of God's hours to settle on a price.

Once back in Endland Jonesey took his time to adjust, weighing up his prospects, and indeed since the labour market had changed people all over were keen to hire an O level telepath and Negative Futurist like him. He worked for business mainly, in dusty offices, backrooms and archives.

All he had to do was pass his hands over a document (like they taught him at niteschool) and he could tell you if the deal was good or not or if the client true, what the small print felt like, what invisible clauses there were and if the devil or devils lived deep in the hearts of the men what had perpetrated the deal. Some days he dint even have to see the paperwork but could just smell the client and know how things would turn out.

Some persons have accused that these writings are full of narrational gaps and sudden perplexing changes of topic brought abt by my total failure to appreciate that the reader does not share important vital background information which I possess. However it is my intention to continue regardless.

#

The unexploded bomb lay right under Jonesey's pillow and he did not dare move and attempt to remove it. Instead he just had to lie there and wait for help.

While he waited certain scenes of his life flashed through his head—there was his first kiss with a 'real' woman, there was his car crash (tedious and teenage) and there was the time he planted a shard of lite-bulb in the street outside his bedroom window and a street-lamp had grown, pushing through the molten tarmac and twisting up to the sky, a strange 300w yellow to its colour and a deep 'spook/shimmer' to its glare.

There are those that accuse me of being unable to use language in either of its symbolic or conceptual kinds of meaning, and still others who believe that I cannot grasp or formulate the properties of objects in the abstract, that I cannot raise the question 'why' regarding real happenings, nor can I deal with fictitious situations or comprehend their rationale. Nonetheless I must set down the events.

#

Towards the end of his life Jonesey got in a strange habit of being fearful just before he slept. He panicked as sleep came close to him, mistaking her warm embrace for the cold one of death. He hired a manservant to read his newspaper for him and cross out all references to physical extinction or the mortal nature of man. If a single word on this topic slipped thru the net he went through hours and hours of despondency and sobbing like a child.

In his very last weeks Jonesey sewed money into the lining of his pyjamas lest he should sleepwalk in the night and end up far from home. Pound coins he put in there and dollar bills, some Zloty and some Deutschmarks—never sure, of course, where he might end up if he walked.

I do not know if Jonesey saw this money as taxi-fare home or as cash to pay the dark ferryman what is painted on Heavy Metal album covers but in any case his pyjamas were found one night in the Texas Homebase car-park and all of the money was gone.

I remember the frost, the cold. Cars crushed. Jonesey's voice. People flying. And human kisses. That's all.

Killing of Frank

a good bad life in
eleven short parts

Frank lived in some North England town known only by the title: SELF PITY CAPITAL OF EUROPE. What pissed Frank off was that someone kept throwing stone tablets down the well behind his council house. Them tablets were inscribed with all kind of foul curses and being as how the well was deep they ended up right near the underworld where God or the Gods might surely act upon them, at least if you believed in that kind of thing.

#

Poor Frank—he was up at all hours of the day and nite trying to fish the tablets out of the well and his breakfast table was nothing but a big mess of breakfast cereal packets and stone tablets drying in electrical light.

MURDEROUS FUCK & POISON TO FRANK said the tablets.

PAX AMERICANA.

NEGATIVE STRIPAGRAM FOR ANYONE WHAT LIVES HERE.

#

Frank's neighbour was an American delegate to the recent peace talks, staying at Mrs Pottage's B&B and dealing crack cocaine as a sideline.

Frank kept offering the bloke money to see if he would help catch the scum what was throwing curses in his well but the Yankee was a filthy reluctant coward. Each nite you could see him counting his money and watching that rubbish movie STREETS OF YESTERDAY on tv.

#

Month after month the peace talks dragged on and it really seemed like Cromwell, King Arthur, Richard The Lion Hunt (sic) and the Reading Chapter of Hells Angels would never make a truce with the govt or anyone else they were fighting.

Stuck in town for no reason, Jake (the bloke from the US delegation) slowly made a friend of Frank and other local persons in the local pub.

#

Over many pints of local lager beer, J kept saying how he wanted to go home and how he just wished the war would end. So far as he was concerned in fact, just cos there were a few kids still throwing stones at tanks in Toxteth, it really didn't constitute a war anymore.

Not by his definition.

J's room at Mrs Pottage's was full of books of philosophy, law, war and killing—so if anyone should've known about wars etc it was him.

#

Anyway. One nite Frank persuaded J to sit with him and watch the well and they talked, and listened to the radio a bit.

Frank had purchased one of those guns which people had in movies—a gun that could fire any number of bullets you wanted until the final moment of tension when it would run out. He kept the gun inside his Adidas bag which still bore the names of teen groups he had scrawled and loved during puberty.

BABY BIRD it said. GOAT TRAILER.

POISON JAMES.

#

Sat by the well in 'cool November breeze' © and waiting, J talked a lot of shit like how he was a difficult person to befriend and he was always moving on from one war to another etc and blah blah. J's hair smelt of 'ambulances in the moonlight' ©, he talked about death, taxes and the devil and how he'd once seen Arthur Scargill's blue movie Cameo.

Each night when he slept, at least if you believed J, he dreamed that someone was trying to barcode-scan his eyes. This kind of talk made Frank feel stupid.

#

Round midnight the well-vandal came—a mysterious figure who looked from a distance like an old Hindu woman in full purdah but who turned out to be a gangly white teenager in a snorkel parka.

The kid was called POORLY APPOINTMENT HEALTH INSURANCE KASMER and Frank took a shot at him as he walked toward the well. Frank shot and he kept shooting but the kid KASMER kept coming, like the

bullets couldn't stop him (i.e. drugs). J panicked
and ran for cover in a nearby house.

                              #

Time is always and only Timex.

As KASMER got closer Frank kept shooting (wow,
like, maybe 36 shots from a pistol!) until just
then of course his gun ran out and the kid still
wasn't dead. KASMER got right up to Frank and then
sunk a knife in him, going right thru his check
shirt and his lucky nude-woman playing cards,
right into his heart.

With Frank dead on the paving slabs KASMER
walked off and dropped his last curse tablet in
the well.

BEATLES RE-FORM IN YOUR GARDEN it said.

PISS ON THE FLAG.

                              #

At home that night KASMER watched tv. Atom bombs
had been dropped on some cities but the news was
confusing. RANK XEROX had bought up all the legal
rights to the words GROUND ZERO and whenever anyone
said them they had to say GROUND XEROX © instead
or else face prosecution, persecution and jail.

"GROUND XEROX © for the explosion was at such
and such a place..." the newsreaders kept saying
and "Now, here's a report from Martin Banham at
GROUND XEROX © ..." etc.

KASMER poured himself a beer and sneered—

people made money out of anything these days.

#

Across town some cops were lounging around shooting their guns at an old canister of POPCRASH. These cops were in a cushy squad whose job it was to turn up late, just after all the action was over, sirens blaring and brakes screeching. If they did well on this squad they sometimes got transferred to another squad where they dint ever have to turn up at all—only turn the sirens on in the distance to let people know they were around.

These cops were arseholes.

Round 1AM they got a call abt the stabbing of Frank. The lead cop jumped in his car and they all roared off. Frank was long dead when they arrived and their sirens were blaring.

Carmen
by Bizet

Many times in the night Carmen is woke up from sleep by the phone ringing but there is no person at the other end with a voice to talk to her, just electronic noise of 'night'. It goes on for months and months. She can't sleep, can't sleep: the phone rings, she answers and when she does get to it there's just this screeching, white hiss of dreams from hell, all electric.

Anyway. After culture of complaint etc etc the black bloke from the telephone company comes around and sits in her house for a night to decipher. Carmen sleeps a bit but feels funny with him sitting about in the other room. Sleep comes slowly, or not at all; when she gets up in the morning he is still there where she left him—at the table, a pack of nudist cards dealed out in front of him.

He says, "Some sort of electronic device is trying to communicate with your telephone". But he offer no more explanation than that. He leaves. Carmen cries.

#

For a while Carmen gives up on answering the phone at all, ignoring all calls in an attempt to banish demons. But this don't work of course. She has to start answering agen in the end.

The breakthru comes one mighty nite. She has been drinking. The phone rings and she answers again—her ears meet the same fucked up tune—the white noise of black dreams at 9600 kbs—and this time, for the 1st time, she understands it.

Revelation(s). Like in the religious book. (5 letters, beginning with 'B'.)

Carmen sits transfixed, listening to the screech, squall, chaos of data loony tune—but her ears deciphering it and her 'bad heart' © thrilling to the words.

#

Whatever it is at the other end tells Carmen a story. She tinks (Irish slang for thinking) of it like a garbled, unwritable chronicle of Endland (sic)—an error message from history—with no holds barred, no tapes erased, no folders shredded in the basement of it.

#

Voice says:

...a cavalcade of lying adulterous politicians and dead princesses, a landscape thru which 24 screen multiplexes multiply unchecked...

Carmen listens, her arms wrapped around herself, like a parcel wrapped too tite, stood in the kitchenette of her flatlet, stood still on linoleum tiles.

...the execution of Queen Elizabeth II, the ascension to Heaven of Bobby Sands, the millennium stripathon televised live to the nation, the brutal decimalisation of time with its

consequences now so familiar to us all...

Dawn approaches. Slogans haunt the noise—words: LONG HAUL, NIGGERS OUT and HOTEL BINARY. The word SUBLIMINALISSIMO!, a t-shirt with the slogan: LOVE IS THE DRUG, BEER IS THE CURE.

Carmen listens and listens (3 months) and when the pigs (cops) finally come round and throw her out the flat for non-payment of rent and ignorance of the BRITISH LAW, she is still hooked into the phone, listening and whispering.

#

Carmen in court.

In a grip of a legal system more vicey and corrupt than anythin what Charles 'Costume Drama' Dickens could have even cooked up. West Midlands Serious Crime Squad in charge of her case, security more tite than in H block and the barristers defending her play a lot of wordgames to keep themselves amused when showing off their closing remarks. They are bored rich people waiting to go home to double-barrel names.

One of them (a woman called _____) is stood up talking. The other banisters pass her a note —whatever words it says on that note, she has to incorporate into her remarks to the jury. Ha ha. At first it is not too hard: she has to incorporate the words 'jurisdiction' and 'responsibility' and 'chromoesome' (sic) (this last slightly harder). But as the day wears on the demands of the game get harder and harder. (Each game pushes to its edges). Her colleagues pass a note which bears the words 'guilty as scum' and 'congenital liar'. Hard to include these words without casting aspersions. The jury send Carmen down for a good long time.

#

Carmen in jail.

She misses her friend the 'electronic device of some kind'; she dreams of him/it/her, like many persons do. Its thick voice calling in the 'nite'.

Carmen whispers the same strange language— thick electrics, background sound—when she is lying in her bed, when she is working in the mail room. Other inmates tag her strange but a few tune in to her oral history. Inmates/intimates. Carmen says there is medicine for people like her but she won't take it.

She speaks of the deregularisation of everything. Of the resinking of the Titanic. She speaks of the time that the soldiers came in the middle of the night and rounded up the whole 'British Happy Family of Showbiz' and shot them all—Tarby clinging to 'Babs' Windsor, Chris Evans, Wolf Man, Shane Richie, Leg Blackston, Paula, Brucie, Pinky and Parky, Emma Thompson and the other one and Sting and Sunny Peterson and all the rest of them in deep shitpop—as the cattle trucks tucked them into oblivion of roadside shallow graves.

Imagine the scene, like that bit in 'The Greaty ESCAPE' (PAL EuroVision X Cert): they all get let out to 'stretch legs', Lenny Henry is talking to some old timer (R____) and the cops (pigs) put the guns on a tripod and mow the fuckers down. ("I done the earth a favour...")

#

Carmen asleep.

In the dream she tries to draw an outline of the nation (Endland). Green eyes frank with 'concentration' ©.

But the biro-shape she makes changes, amoeba-like, shifting and pulsing, some science experiment (a biology class in Winter 1989)—incorporation of cities, demolition of borders, erosion of space-time—trams in the streets, Tsars re-instated—Walt Disney a symbolic head of state.

Fed up of white noise. You don't even know your OWN history how can I tell you mine?

The dream comes to an abrupt end, a videofit man pointing a sawn-off shotgun at Carmen (the angel of death that haunts all of them dreams, everybody knows the routine). C sticks her thumb in the barrel of it (the shotgun) to stop the explosion...the bullets fire, the gun swells rapidly, bursts, showering soot on the shooter and noise in the bedroom/jailcell of her morning.

Everytime I try to write gun I write gin.
Endland DREAMING.

#

Carmen loses her name. In jail they call her
DEATH.

One night C/D leaves her cell—slipping between
the bars like anorexics can.

The phone in the hallway rings.

She answers it. Not really thinking 'guess
who'—as obvious to her as it is to anyone else.

White noise on the phone.

(By accident I am typing white noose, or white
nose...)

01111 10000 100090100100010111100 0110
010101010000 101010 0101010100 101010 0010
01010101010100000101010000001011101101010101010
01010100 01010 01010 0101010 01000010101010101101
010101010 10101111001010101010101001000010101
011110101011110100111000111001101010 0101

#

What the phone call said.

History of Endland continued in 26 illus
episodes. Vile threats and early closing, free
binders and 2 dogs locked up in back of cars.
Shoot to kill and free milk. 2 idiots living in
a museum. Because septic pub shit, because weather
and sex in an igloo tent, sick in a chemical
toilet and "reform" of "welfare" "state" (word for

faeces, four letters, C-something-A-something).

Because fucked up. And pushing 50. And classical class system and stunt your desire and don't you know don't you know don't you know, stealing grave tributes to build a weird shrine in the house. Because of an equation between boys with motorbikes. Because girls are defined in the first place by a lack. Because streetlamps and long motorway journeys and because Elvis only stopped here on the way to somewhere else. Because Drug Squad stake out @ Leicester Forest East. Because Service Stations of the Cross. Because. Because. Because. Remember that story you read of as a child, saying: if women are a mystery then men are a crime story.

#

Miranda. (WRONG NAME).

Carmen. Carmen stood in the hallway of Holloway. Hell of Hallway. Listening to the phone.

EnDLAND. cut. paste.

0111101010111101001110001110011010100101

#

NO SUCH THING AS STORIES JUST A COLLECTION OF INDIVIDUALS.

Each game pulls twds its own edges.

Each body also.

#

Because exploded, because Xploded.

Because.

You a bunch of liars and murderers.

Listen to 'sad music' © in your night. Forget about anything.

Because sentimental panto piano tunes. Cheggers plays pop. Karaoke bar with insects.

Ever have the feeling?

#

Carmen. CAR. MEN.

Funny mane (name) if u break it down like that.

Got the shits. Got the shots.

Got the hump. Got the bone. Got the point.

Got the loss.

Got nothing.

Got lost.

Carmen.

#

TELL THIS STORY TO ALL YOUNG CHILDREN ANYWHERE.

Tell them how she walked past the last street lamp and into the dark or got in a taxi and never 'was' again.

That's the real jailbreak.

Tell your kids that the voice they hear in the cellar is hers, that the night voice is hers, that what they hear from the wardrobe in their hurtable hurtable dreams is Carmen whispering, Carmen talking on, with her whisper of Endland's blood and history.

TELL THEM CARMEN comes to get those kids that never do their homework.

Tell them that.

Tell them anything.

Tell them this:

THE HUMAN SOUL IS NOTHING BUT A BAR-CODE.

ISBN 1-901072-12-6

9 781901 072129

A dead man's eyes are a curse to those that behold them.

I am gone from here.

I am out of here, man.

I say: later guys, later.

The pub fills up with miners, whippets, pit-bulls and prole new home-owners.

Bloke at the bar says "Oh fuck, it's really starting to stink of realism in here"

The travellers pull on their antiquated hats and capes. They exeunt.

Carmen (a remix) is playing on the fruitmachine.

TELL THIS STORY TO ALL KIDS ANYWHERE.

Call it a historectomy of Endland (sic).

A BAD NIGHT LIFE IN ONE SHORT PART

German Fokker

When great chart fame and fortune came to the talentless crooner Fokker in his 25th yr, his whole life took on that dire air and weight of bad pop video, all things done cheap and surreal. Living in Manchester, Endland (sic) his girls were anorexic would-be sphinxes, his house was full of pigeons, doves or waterfalls and each nite before he slept mixed-race blokes in silver jumpsuit type outfits would mouth glistening incomprehensible words on top of a brite green hill near his housing estate.

Of course the bastard council sent people round, complaints abt noise and animal treatment, and a poxy lawsuit followed with some fans what had written Fokker's name and album title on the pavement outside his door. Managers and agents hassled Fokker, calling him up all time when he just wanted to sleep and go down in slow motion with his mates.

If all that crap were 'the price of fame' © Fokker was soon bored—a lifetime's ambition burned up in weeks nearly—the stupid turd growing old before his time, not really liking life. So what if his 'new record' was number three (3) in a chart or if some big lawyer and quantity control bloke from Mexico wanted to see him. On a typical day he (a) could not get his tv to sit straight on the lilo, (b) got a leak in his waterbed and (c) spent all nite riding thru rain in some dickhead car looking for a big rave in a field what turned out to be cancelled.

One night at his house and at the height of his boredom and fame an angel came to Fokker in a dream and told him he had to go to LAZARUS, a club in Rotherham where a bloke had died and then come back. Lazarus was a DJ now it seemed and played slow beats slower than the devil himself.

Guestlist, stretch pants and shirt by Stephen Berkoff, Fokker got a black cab to LAZARUS where he got out of the door (of the cab) and put each of his feet on the pavement, one by one, lifting them and then putting them down repeatedly and thus moving forwards until he got to the door. Sometimes it seemed now that even the simplest things were difficult for Fokker.

Kids in the club recognised Fokker but were too cool to say owt, whispering the name of his band and latest crap-concept album. In centre of the room a gang of 1st Div footballers in elaborate glam drag were dancing round a pile of handbags belonging to their wives or girlfriends. This were a strange scene indeed, made stranger by the lighting all of a puke greenish hue. At edges of the room were more dancers on scaffolding and a booth where the DJs were. Inside that booth which was mentioned before an old looking Japanese bloke was talking over the music (never a good thing in a DJ), and describing at some length his experiences on August 13th 1945 in Hiroshima—the way the bomb blast had shook him and the way his skin had seemed for a moment to be of translucent colour and how he had even seen rite thru his bones. Of all this talking no one batted an eyelid at it but Fokker couldn't quite get hip to the beat—maybe the Jap rapper was all part of the LAZARUS idea he thought—other blokes who'd nearly died doing PA's in the club or something, the odd allnighter in a mortuary, Fokker didn't know anyhow, and, being German, had no sense of humour whatsoever about anything.

After a long time the Jap bloke stopped talking and the slow beat theme carried on with a less than catchy tune sounding like a mixture of late Kray Twins and early Hawker Siddley. Footballers left the dancefloor in a hurry and it soon thronged full with daft twats showing off to straight girls waiting to get married and play housey housey.

Fokker nodded to some people he thought he probably knew but didn't and bought a packet of fags from a machine in the corner by the bogs, getting strange looks from a group of kids what were lurking in its shadow and who until recently had had their heads buried in polythene bags full of glue. Fokker was exactly that sort of bloke what slept in the daytime and went out in the 'nightime' © but even he had to admit 'true cause' that the niteclub LAZARUS was weird:

—A tv in the corner showed a boxing match with Joe DiMaggio.

—A poster on the wall was for a new boy-band called FAECES.

—Two ex-miners were stood at the bar discussing the ill-fortune of their various video shops, opened on redundancy cash in 85 and now getting driven into crisis by Blockbuster/Ritz.

A kid on the other side of the cavernous hall caught Fokker's eye and beckoned him over. It was all like that bit on the advert for Cadbury's Chocolate Nooses ® where the tank is rolling past a city skyline in flames, and them soldiers on the gibbet exchange a look of love and laughter and hatred and brotherhood and struggle and passion and hope and understanding and forgiveness and violence and more love and wisdom and guilt and pride for just a few seconds before the trapdoor opens and they fall.

The kid gestured to a chair and bade Fokker sit down, a smile right on his mouth. Hi sed Fokker, hi sed the kid and Fokker palmed a little bottle of drugs the kid handed him and, after 'sundry chit chat' and 'mouthing off for no reason' ©, he slipped off to the loo. In the bogs a black girl from New York was selling hairspray, condoms, combs and other crap, all laid out on a makeshift cardboard-box table. A bloke was pissing in the urinal and talking to his mate but, since looking down at his dick in strange concentration, now totally unaware that his mate had long gone.

"Yeah," he was saying as Fokker stumbled out of

his cubicle, the drug starting to work in him already. "Marion and I hev sold de house and are goin up country for an little while. I want to live right out of there man, I mean right out there, where de air is clean you know and de Insomnia is pure..."

Fokker only read the label on the bottle (of drugs) after he had taken it all, which is not really the most sensible way to do it but it works for some people. HEROINE it said on the bottle (when he did bother to read it) and indeed it wasn't long before one arrived—a skinny girl in a very short pastel skirt, a black and white top and a thin gold chain glinting round her tanned exposed midriff. Hi sed Fokker and she sed hi back proving at least that conversation was not yet dead in the country of Endland (sic). Her name, it transpired, was Miranda.

Lowered from the ceiling on his bed Lazarus entered the DJ booth in flamboyant style and started his second set. There was the sound of choppers in the air outside the club or tent or whatever and rumours that police (the pigs) were arresting the whole queue of people outside. Everyone inside didn't seem to mind. Lazarus put a record or two on—one by Abba and the other by Slade—but he couldn't seem to get people dancing. He put on more tunes—by Heater and by Nobody and by Rolf Harris and so on—so soon there was five (5) songs all playing at the same time. Fokker was more a singer/crooner than a back-from-the-dead DJ type but even he could see that Lazarus was good, if a little clumsy on the turntable and unorthodox in his methods.

When folks did get moving you couldn't exactly tell if maybe it was for Coldstream Guards or The Belsen or Smokey but anyway when they did get moving it were like L could do no wrong etc playing the crowd like it were a music instrument of which he had the absolute master race blah blah. Fokker kept watching, his eyes 'wide'. Just when it looked like 'quite a good do' tho, Lazarus cut the mood and went into a long long slow rap about life before death and life after death and other crap, clearing the floor. Only Miranda in the whole club and the whole world danced to this Lazarus rap—snaking and turning slowly in the middle of the dancefloor all alone while Fokker watched her from the rail and a crowd of black blokes made a circle round her and wolf whistling, clapping their hands and nodding wisely at the good dancing.

It was sometime in Miranda's dance that Fokker started to feel a bit funny and strange like the HEROINE was really pretty strong, maybe cut with something, maybe not. He had the impression (like the poets say) that he was drunk and 'sinking and rising at the same time' © and later he saw a vague hallucination of a zebra up amongst party decorations in the club roof. When he checked his watch (a really good one which seemed to have a M. Mouse face and everything) he found it had slowed and then, only moments later, stopped. The slow beats were indeed running very slow that nite, Lazarus well into his groove and all kids in the club creeping about like their very feet were the royalty of whispering.

Fokker watched Miranda dance, her hands pulling colours from the air but when he felt too weird he looked round vaguely for the bloke what sold him the HEROINE to ask him (1) what the fuck it was and (2) how long it lasted and (3) if there were probably any dangerous side effects etc, but he couldn't see him. Too late. Even the footballers seemed wild and other-worldly now, just barely recognisable behind the large pyramid of beer glasses they had built, Bobby Moore and Arthur Ramsey laughing uproariously at David Platt who was sinking a third pint while a fourth (4th) one was balanced on his head.

Miranda danced—flat stomach, her arms snakes, eyes black of nothing, slow beats so slow that when Fokker checked his pulse, leaned against a pillar he could not find it at all, dark closing in at the edges of his vision.

For one moment he thought he saw the lights of the club swim, shift and combine to tell him a message, moving slowly into focus with Miranda in the centre but then Lazarus changed his groove again and the beats slowed even more, some track by Freud about the uncanny, with a riff on heimlich/unheimlich, heimlich/unheimlich, a chill of ice in the air and Fokker went falling to the floor in so very many pieces.

Three weeks later F woke up in a hospital going cold turkey from HEROINE. The girl missing and despite all enquiries like no one knew her, no one saw her and no one even registered her name. Of the bloke what dealt him the drug no sign neither. Fokker wept on tabloid tv, did interviews from intensive care and, like OJ Simpson promising to catch the real killer of Nicole Brown, he promised that he too (once better) would scour the real world only looking for Miranda.

Fokker needn't have bothered though. One nite while he was sleeping on the ward she came back to him, in costume of a nurse and she danced for him again and while she danced he glimpsed his heartbeat on the EEG, the spikes and beats of it slowing, rippling, slowing, like real slow beats, lime green spikes on dark green ground, Miranda dancing and Fokker saw the lines on the EEG go crazy for a moment, spike beat, skip beat and then ripple and then turn into birds, the birds flying over the screen, lime green birds on dark green ground, wings beating slowly slowly and then gone.

FOKKER DEAD ran the headlines next day.

GIRL MISSING.

ENDLAND DREAMING.

Fokker's album went double platinum and his manager got rich.

The Life, Movies &
Short Times of
Natalie Gorgeous

Everyone knows that Natalie Gorgeous was born in Milan. But not everyone knows that her uncle owned a shoe factory and that her aunt once went to Venice in the hope of being a model but came back broke and exhausted after a month.

The story of how Natalie was discovered—while playing in a fountain in the Rue De Jules Verne—is also well known. Natalie was seventeen, the man who found her was Varese Sarbande, an octogenarian film-producer who lived most of his life in hotels.

#

Natalie's first film, in 1964, was an immediate success, starring as she did in the Oscar-winning GORGEOUS IN LOVE (MGM). The film, a delightful sentimental comedy, broke box office records that year, competing with the surprise international hit NIGHT OF CRUSHER (Soviet Kino) and with another debut feature, this time for Crude Laverne, who took the starring role in Paul Goddard's sexually explicit picture BLUE VEIN FOR ELLEN (Raunch Productions).

#

If competition at the box office began a problematic rivalry between Gorgeous and Laverne, it was not helped by the press and publicity departments of their respective studios or by persistent rumours of their shared (and unrequited) love for a handsome Russian stage-actor Yuri Gagarin.

1965 saw Natalie Gorgeous make two films—the first a slight romantic comedy titled GORGEOUS KNOWS BEST (MGM) and the second her classic action thriller GORGEOUS IN THE RAIN (FOX). This latter film made a name for Natalie Gorgeous all over the world, establishing her forever in the firmament of international stars. Few people in the developed or developing worlds cannot repeat line for line the final gripping and tempestuous dialogue between Gorgeous and her co-star Paul Trajectory, a dialogue which won the hearts of a whole generation and left Natalie with a catchphrase which would follow her until death: "We're in a strange land, baby, and going to a worse land..."

#

The years 64 and 65 were years of long parties, studio dinners, endless photocalls, interviews and romances. They were not, however, without their difficulties. Catapulted to true stardom after GORGEOUS IN THE RAIN, Natalie experienced many of the problems faced by other beautiful and talented young women in her position. Her stony and brittle love affairs (with producer Sven Hassel, actor Kurt Jaw and the writer Peter Barlow) are as well documented as her increasing reliance on drink and the fringes of prescription medication to cope with the pressures of life at the top.

Her films of the period 1966-1969 range from the predictable GORGEOUS WITH A GUN, through the unexpected propaganda effort about women in the coal industry titled GORGEOUS UNDERGROUND to the classic comedy BED TIME FOR GORGEOUS.

Only in this later movie, teamed once again with actor Paul Trajectory and with writer Nicholas Copernicus, did Gorgeous live up to the promise of her early performances—breaking hearts all over Christendom with her rendition of the title song.

#

While Gorgeous floundered slightly in the mid to late sixties, her rival Crude Laverne scored a series of enormous hits (no pun intended) with movies such as BIG GIRLS DON'T HAVE TO TRY (MGM), CRUDE OIL (Smeltdown) and the classic of wide-screen erotica WIDE OPEN (Lumiere Pictures). Indeed some shots in this last film were reckoned so realistic that audiences in Paris (by all accounts) came running from the cinema in fear and surprise as Laverne approached the camera for the first time.

1970 saw Natalie Gorgeous making the first of her comebacks, the story of which and of her whirlwind romance and marriage to the round-the-world yachtsman Dennis Sony need no further elaboration. The book written by her hairdresser GREGORIOUS ON GORGEOUS (Pan Publications) provides a touching, if at times libellous account of these years. 1970-74 saw no less than nine Gorgeous movies including the chiller thriller GORGEOUS ON ICE, the thriller romance THE TRUTH ABOUT GORGEOUS, the romantic espionage drama GORGEOUS UNDERCOVER and the made for tv kung fu chiller FISTS OF GORGEOUS.

#

If things looked good for Natalie in this period they did not stay looking good for long. The tragic accident which struck Dennis Sony during his voyage across the Atlantic, the death (from a Tamazepan overdose) of her close friend and confidante Evelyn Pascal and her long and bitter lawsuit with her management company (Galileo PLC) all took their toll.

Fate was no more kind to Crude Laverne whose brief incarceration in a Birmingham mental hospital was followed by a succession of dire flops at the box office in half-hearted and lack-lustre exploitation movies like SEX HOTEL, SEX MOTEL, SEXY HOTEL, SEXY MOTEL and SEX HOTEL II. If once she'd raised the temperature of Europe and America, Laverne, it seemed now, could only just raise the rent on her 5th Avenue apartment and her engagement to director Romeo Giggle was broken off.

#

Tastes in Hollywood and Cannes changed and by 1976 Natalie Gorgeous was no longer the box office star she had once been. The days when her very presence in a restaurant was more or less sufficient cause to close it and where her visits to a town were followed night and day by the mobilisation of a shadow army of press, photographers, news-crews and admirers were also gone.

For Natalie, periods of semi-retirement (skiing in Italy, walking the hills in Scotland, dating the American actor—and later president—Neil Armstrong) were followed by occasional comebacks in made for tv mini-series and straight to video releases. These films have only Natalie to recommend them and even the most cursory watching of say GORGEOUS IN THE GULAG (Turner Entertainment 1977) or GORGEOUS IS FOREVER (Viacom 1978) show a woman whose talent far outshines the material with which she is forced to work.

#

Readers seeking even the briefest history of the Third World War would do well to look beyond this volume, but events of such great magnitude touch the lives of the biggest stars and the lowliest public alike. In the aftermath of the bombings in Paris, Reykjavik and Canterbury and the brief atomic jihad which followed them, Gorgeous, like many others, took refuge in the neutral countries —fleeing to Sweden, Finland, and even Imperial

Russia before settling in Bosnia Herzegovnia in 1980. As the world licked its wounds and began the task of rebuilding, Natalie Gorgeous became a recluse, refusing work, public appointments, interviews and requests for photographs on the rare occasions that people succeeded in tracking her down.

Only her daughter Helena (a love child born to Natalie and the Las Vegas singer Peter Tarkovsky) stayed in the public eye, appearing at the New Cannes Festival to attend the premier of Crude Laverne's successful come-back movie OLDER WOMAN (Medina Films)—as if, in the fullness of time, and like the great feuds of world geo-politics and ideology, even the old movie-star feuds had to be settled.

#

After 1978, as is well known, Natalie Gorgeous made only one appearance on film, shunning even an invitation from Bakunin to join him in the Far East where the Oscar committee were holding a small dinner in Gorgeous' honour. Natalie had deserted the celluloid stage, it seemed at least, forever.

It was left to Julian Schroeder, a young German film-maker fresh out of film school, to capture Natalie Gorgeous' swan-song. Conceived as a final examination project and made on a minimal budget his LAST TRAIN TO GORGEOUS (Zoetrope 1996) was an epic journey across re-constructing Europe by train. Lasting 7 hours and fifteen minutes in its complete version, the film (shot on a mixture of super-8 and low-band video) is both a homily to Natalie and the films she has made and a vision of the new world emerging from the old, an essay on the possibilities of life and love in the 1990's. Visiting the locations for many of her most famous performances, LAST TRAIN TO GORGEOUS also takes in some of the most extraordinary scenes of life in post-nuclear Europe, including documentary footage from the work-camps in Belgrade, the shelters in Coventry and Versailles and the vast unspeakable wreckage of Euro-Disney. With its text by the young Tim Etchells and its soundtrack by Laibach in collaboration with the ageing US composer William Shatner, LAST TRAIN TO GORGEOUS is a memorable enough experience for anyone and yet to mention these things at all is to lessen our focus on the film's final and absolutely focal moments.

#

Arriving in Sarajevo the film-maker Julian Schroeder seeks out the house of Natalie Gorgeous. It is the moment for which we have been waiting (implicitly and explicitly) the whole seven hours of the film, and it will not disappoint us, however brief this final encounter may be.

Schroeder walks up a frostbitten and overgrown

path, through a series of rusted iron gates, past statues dark with loss and lichen—weeping angels, twisted gargoyles of the late twentieth century. He comes to a door, a heavy wooden door to a house which seems part fairy tale cottage and part fairy tale castle (all this merely glimpsed on the walk to the porch) and the camera is just behind him, carried on the shoulders of his assistant Steve Rogers who has been with Schroeder on the whole trip.

Schroeder knocks on the door. There is a long wait and a silence. We can see Schroeder's breath in the morning air and we can see that his breath is uneven and he's just about to knock again when the door opens, taking him by surprise and bringing our seven hours and fifteen minutes of waiting to an end. Natalie Gorgeous is standing in the doorway, in a black dress, with her hair down and her eyes as lively and intense as they have ever been and she looks at the camera, as only she can—somewhere between nothingness and the knowing of everything.

And then, just as her eyes catch the camera, in the micro-seconds of our knowing once again her gaze, after so many years, after so many hours, the film begins to fade, slowly at first and then more rapidly, so that in a count of three seconds she is gone, never to be seen again, not ever, ever, ever. And we are left with the voices of Schroeder and Rogers, explaining who they are and

why they have come, voices that also fade out, as
the credits roll in a rich black and blankness
that is only an absence of Natalie Gorgeous.

APPENDIX

—Natalie Gorgeous (1946-1996)

Filmography:

A full filmography of Natalie Gorgeous will be added in a later
edition.

—Crude Laverne (1947-)

At the time of writing Crude Laverne is still alive and living
in Occupied London with her husband and two children from a
previous marriage.

Filmography:

A full filmography of Crude Laverne will be added in a later
edition.

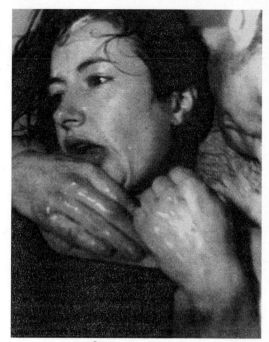

Arse on
Earth

One of the Gods whose name shall be nameless and who is not known for his feministic point of view takes several lovers: one called Mouth whose job it is to suck him off, one called Arse whose rectum is his one source of enjoyment in her body, another called Titties and still another called Legs and so on and so forth.

After a while the other Gods get right fed up with this bloke and his bad behavioural attitude and they threaten to ban him from the All Olympian Playing Fields wherein they roam.

Of course this does no good. The days and nights pass with an orgy of handwringing while the naughty (errant) God takes even more lovers named after body-parts and his continual fracturisation of the female-type corpus creates an oppressive atmosphere for everyone (blah blah blah). IFOR get called in, for all that ever achieves.

#

Anyway. Quite independent of the so-called 'moral issue' ©, Arse decides to run away. She is fed up with the treatment meted out to her by the nameless God——she has other orifices after all and 'needs' and 'desires' just like the rest of us—— and she descends to earth in the guise of an ordinary woman, determined to forge a new 'life' there.

This story is the tale of her adventures. Of what she found on earth and what she liked about it. Of her pleasures and perils and, sadly, how in the end she contrived to answer the question: WHY IS MODERN LIFE RUBBISH?

#

Arse came down to Derby in North Endland (sic). It was winter and the govt was organising a cull of many pigeons in the city. All the way round it men in gasmasks were squirting that yellow gas into the bare trees where pigeons had gathered and then (as the dumb dead pigeons fell) they were clearing them all up and making big bonfires, spurred on by union negotiated overtime, bloodlust and kerosene.

Enough already.

Arse put her name down for a council flat and soon she got a job in a local Cash & Carry that mainly sold knock-down bargain basement pornography at bulk-only prices. She had no friends to speak of and knew little of the ways of earth. If you looked at her in the street she might have looked like a case of care in the community or like someone who has lost something but who has forgotten what it is that they have lost.

What seemed strange about Earth? The colours— brighter than she expected. The many many sounds —somehow louder and more varied. The sound of someone laughing in the road outside.

#

Arse wakes repeatedly in the early hours of morning. Not exactly jet-lag or problems adjusting to time zones but the kind of lag that happens when you come down from Heaven onto Earth —the lag that some people call Melancholy. She is constantly awake in the pre-dawn cold. She is constantly thinking about writing a letter to _____. She is constantly nervous with butterflies in her stomach.

Often on these mornings, in the far far distance she hears the ringing of car alarms in the city beyond—a soft sound that soon she grows to love as others might love the sound of 'oceans' © or of 'wind machines' ©.

Arse starts work on a questionnaire—not so much market research as a personal attempt to keep track of her feelings about life on earth.

#

Her key questions:
WHERE DO DREAMS COME FROM?
WHY ARE PEOPLE SCARED OF THE DARK?
CAN YOU LOVE A PLACE AND HATE IT AT THE SAME TIME?

#

At work Arse were mostly on checkouts—a fallen Goddess sat beneath the vast sky of fluorescent striplights with a name badge on her pinkish nylon coverall. Time passed slowly, or not at all.

On Mondays Arse got switched to the loading bay

and she and 'the daft lads what worked there' helped customers stack up their vans and cars with all boxes of pornographic stuff. She liked that Monday work more—it was physical and, if not exactly farming, at least semi-out-of-doors.

Life in the shop (HOUSE OF TOSS) was different to what she was used to—no more Olympian Brand Food, no more sweet gentle music from the harp of Vesuvius or Volpone or Varese or whoever and no more getting fucked up the rectum.

Some days indeed, when business was really slow, Arse and the daft lads would open up them sealed packages of PLAYDOUGH, stare at the picture-spreads in BREAST IMPLANT MONTHLY and then, feeling strong (or in any case enormously desensitised) descend to the top shelf and the dubious pleasures of WOMB RAIDERS II.

It was in HOUSE OF TOSS that Arse learned the true meaning of human love, the ways of money, tax, healthcare schemes and National Insurance. And, when she had learned those things, she left.

#

The months after TOSS passed quickly and our heroine sought other employment of a full or part time nature more fitting to her personage.

She went for jobs at Asda, at Kall-Kwik and at Bullet-Proof Versace. She didn't get any of them and soon she ended up working at a bar called TITS & ASS and there was a lot of very many predictable jokes from the customers concerning her name along lines of "You've got a nice arse, Arse..." and "Arse, don't get all arsey on me..." etc.

Arse suffers months of confusion, working in the bar.

Her dreams are of Heaven, her days a Bosch picture traced out onto skin. Touches, grabs, caresses, jabs, bites, collisions, kisses, scrapes, grazes. Too-brief (or too long) encounters. All written on her.

Fast forward through it—i.e. a whole bunch of stuff about all different people in the bar and what a hard fucking time Arse had and 'stink of poverty' ©. The bright bright colours of earth. The violence of sound. Neon sign outside the bar runs that Coke-slogan KEEP ON FALLING and the red then green then red again figure of an angel falling, neon dancing. Strange to fall from Heaven to such a place as this.

Arse forgets most of what happens to her which is just as well. She keeps trying to write a report on MODERN LIFE (as she calls it) but many of the salient facts are missing.

#

After a time she learns a bit concerning friendship.

One of the other girls that works the bar is called Tiffany. Tiffany and Arse become good friends. Tiffany is from the 'countryside' or possibly from a small town in Lancashire——it's a place no one speaks the name of unless they happen to come from there or unless they get kinda lost on the route to someplace else.

Arse and T move into a house together. Girl intimate. A blue house. With lavender curtains.

T tells Arse about her text-book country-girl childhood: a family of drunken wife- and kid-beaters, strong silent types that could say more with a thrash of the belt or something than they ever could in English language. In return Arse makes up her own childhood——not the one she lived in Olympia, but a miserable fiction based in Burton Upon Trent.

#

Arse and Tiffany fall in love on the night when they've got tickets to see the live recording of the new smash hit Italian comedy-show called SUBLIMINALISSIMO!

On the way they get lost in the huge multi-storey car park under the tv studios. Tiffany breaks her leg in a fall on some oil. They hear fragments of SUBLIMINALISSIMO! floating thru the vent-ducts of the car park. Their eyes meet. There is quite a look between them.

#

Back home the girls 'make love to each other' but that bit got torn out.

Banging on the walls from next door and upstairs.

[THIS SECTION WRITTEN WHILE THE HOUSE WAS UNDER ATTACK FROM A DRUNK.]

At some point in the act of sex that night Tiffany puts her fingers up Arse's arse. She feels something there. Something moving a little. Something unexpected. She's scared.

For days Arse feels uncomfortable down there—a moving, growing feel, an ache. She goes to the doctor's and gets some ultrasound or a scan of some kind.

She is pregnant—only the child is in her anus. And she knows of course that it must be the child of _____ the nameless God up in Heaven.

#

Key questions:
CAN POVERTY BE BEAUTIFUL?
WHICH SENSE DOES A DYING PERSON TEND TO LOSE FIRST?
WHICH GAS IS ALSO KNOWN AS LAUGHING GAS?

#

Arse decides to keep the child. The hospitals etc will not deal with her, considering the whole narrative to be outside the borders, conventions and interests of medicinal science, so Tiffany is midwife, adviser, doctor, partner. They are living on the breadline, the borderline somewhere between the 70's and the 90's, late Twentieth Century.

And in due time the child is born.

Healthy. Perfect. Gorgeous.

They call her 'Winter', because that is the season in which she is born. And that, they hope, will be her temperament.

It is a well known fact that there are more snakes than ladders in the great game of life.

Things go well and then disaster strikes.

Soldiers come in the Spring. Part of the continual skirmishing which afflicts such borders in space and time. They kill Tiffany and Winter. Just a paragraph in the late news—more problems in the border zone, two dead. A bullet goes in Arse but of course she is immortal. Bloody sheets.

Cliched tears for things that are impermanent. The sorrow of the long haul. Survivor despair.

Arse packs her stuff—a few books, a few photographs. God-stuff. The rest she gives away. The flat she douses and burns. Earthly remains.

She goes back to Heaven.

Key questions:

DO YOU EVER GET A DREAM-LIKE FEELING TOWARDS LIFE WHEN IT ALL SEEMS UNREAL?

DO YOU OPENLY AND SINCERELY ADMIRE BEAUTY IN OTHER PEOPLE?

ARE YOU UP-TO-DATE ON CURRENT AFFAIRS?

WHAT IS THE DIFFERENCE BETWEEN NEW LABOUR AND THE
OTHER BLOODY LOT?
CAN YOU TRAVEL IN TIME?

                        #

A welcome home party in the grounds of a fantastic
castle made of clouds. Olympia doing what it does
best—decadence, depravity. Arse talks to Mouth,
Armpits and Tongue—old friends with lots of news
to catch up on. Drunk on pleasure and Alcopops.
She swaps them stories of Earth—her perils there
and joys.

                        #

Last question:
WHY IS MODERN LIFE RUBBISH?

Fill out your answer in not more than 500 words. Use black ink.
Do not write on both sides of the paper. Do not swear.

Tim Etchells is a writer and artist based in Sheffield, Endland ©. He is best known for his work with Forced Entertainment, who have been called "Britain's most brilliant experimental theatre company" (*The Guardian*). In 1997 he co-directed *DIY,* a film for Channel Four which won the Best Short Documentary prize in the San Francisco Film Festival. *Certain Fragments,* a collection of Etchells' theoretical and critical writing on performance, is being published by Routledge in 1999.